$\mathcal{A}$ CANDLELIGHT ROMANCE

CANDLELIGHT ROMANCES

HEART ON HOLIDAY

Elaine Fowler Palencia

A CANDLELIGHT ROMANCE

Published by
Dell Publishing Co., Inc.
1 Dag Hammarskjold Plaza
New York, New York 10017

To My Parents

Dell ® TM 681510, Dell Publishing Co., Inc.

ISBN: 0-440-13476-5

Printed in the United States of America

First printing—December 1980

CHAPTER ONE

Catherine Gray stamped her foot and said once again in very good Spanish, "But it *has* to be here. I saw it go out on the luggage cart in Miami. Please look again."

The airport clerk shrugged indifferently at her insistence and shuffled off, leaving Catherine to consider her next move. She set down her remaining suitcase, leaned against a column, and closed her eyes with weariness. So far her tropical holiday was off to a rocky start. After a long delay in Miami, the plane had stopped in Bogotá, supposedly just long enough to take on passengers. But everyone had been ordered off with no explanation and had been made to sit in a cold, bare waiting room for two hours. Catherine, in a light summer suit, had envied the *bogotanos* in their blanket-weight ponchos, or *ruanas*, as they were called in Colombia. Now, here she was, after a bumpy ride over a forbidding range of the Andes, outside the centuries-old provincial capital of Cali, with half her luggage missing. It was a strange place to be the day

5

after Christmas, but at least her clothing was appropriate, she thought grimly. The heat was oppressive.

"I'm afraid it won't do any good to wait," said a voice beside her. "Your luggage was probably taken off the plane at Bogotá to make room for more important merchandise coming to Cali."

Catherine's eyes flew open. The voice belonged to a trim, well-dressed man whom she had noticed in the waiting room at Bogotá. Her curiosity had been piqued by a white, crescent-shaped scar that cut into the deep tan of his right cheek; but since he had been in first class and she in tourist, there had been no chance during the flight to observe him further.

"But what will I do?" she asked crossly. "How long will they take to send it on here?"

The man tilted his head slightly as if to get a better look at her, and flashed a smile. "You must come from a place where systems work. The suitcase may come today or it may never come. The trick is not to care too much about possessions. Is this your first trip to Colombia?"

"You're teasing me," Catherine said with asperity, "and I hardly think the situation calls for it."

The stranger's smile disappeared, almost too quickly, thought Catherine, and he bowed curtly. "My apologies. Allow me to introduce myself and to explain that I only wished to be of service to a lovely foreigner. I am César Saavedra Solano."

"Catherine Gray. I'm sorry I snapped at you, but everything seems to be going wrong. Yes, it is my first trip to Colombia, or anywhere else for that matter. I mean, I've never been to a foreign country before."

César Saavedra brushed aside her apology with a wave of his hand. "May I ask if anyone is meeting you?"

"That's part of what's going wrong," sighed Catherine. "When the plane was delayed for so long in Miami, I sent a wire to my friends telling them not to meet me, since I didn't know when we would arrive. They would have had to wait for hours."

"Then you must accept a ride with me," César decided. He motioned to a porter who had been loitering hopefully nearby, and threw an order to the baggage clerk, who had returned from his search empty-handed.

"But I can get a taxi!" Catherine protested sharply, watching her lone suitcase and the stranger's heavy leather one disappear into the crowd with the porter, who seemed to know exactly where to take them.

"Yes, I know you can. Your Spanish is quite adequate," retorted César as he turned to go.

"But my other suitcase!"

"You'll be notified," he said smoothly, leaving Catherine no recourse but to fall in step with him.

As they came up to the customs inspection area, Catherine moved ahead to secure her suitcase from the porter, who was caught in the crush of people and boxes waiting to be cleared; but César took her arm firmly. "We go this way," he ordered, steering her past a line of frazzled tourists. The porter hurried behind them.

A fat, rumpled inspector glanced up and broke into a gold-toothed grin. *"Ah, don César. ¿Cómo está?"*

"Bien, gracias, ¿y Usted? La señorita está conmigo."

"Pase, por favor." The inspector waved them by, ignoring the irate remarks from the gaggle of tourists.

Catherine glanced up at her companion in surprise. Who was this don César Saavedra, that he was not subject to ordinary laws? His looks were certainly commanding, she decided as she took in the haughty profile, the dark, flashing eyes, the slight, sardonic curl of the mouth, and the narrow mustache. Far from

7

spoiling his appearance, the scar enhanced an already striking face. His shoulders were broad for a Latin American, or seemed so because of the confident way he carried himself. He moved unhurriedly through the thronged building, yet although Catherine was fairly tall, she had to match one of his strides with two of her own. She guessed he was well-to-do; the faultless cut of his suit and the fine leather of his dress boots bespoke custom workmanship.

Just outside the main doors of the airport they were met by a uniformed chauffeur, who greeted his employer warmly and leaped to take charge of the luggage.

"And he? Has he been waiting for you all these hours?" Catherine demanded as César handed her into the Mercedes.

"Leonardo? Oh, yes. He is supposed to wait," César said absently as he got in beside her and lay back against the luxurious cushions.

Catherine frowned involuntarily, offended by all that this man seemed to take for granted. She supposed that she should enjoy such distinguished companionship and the beauty of the automobile, but the long trip had put her completely out of sorts. She felt positively dowdy in her wilted suit, which reeked with the smoky, chemical odor of the airplane interior. Further, she was annoyed to be indebted to a stranger and not to have a clear idea of where she was going. She wished the ride were over. All she wanted was a long, hot bath and a longer nap.

"So. Where may we take you?"

Catherine roused herself from her reverie to find that the big automobile was idling, awaiting her orders.

"I have the address in my purse. Here. I hope it's not too far out of your way." She removed her jacket, then sat up and forced herself to make conversation.

"I've come to visit an old school friend of mine, María Lucía Imbert, whose father owns a large factory here, I believe. She has begged me to come for ages but until now I never seemed to have the time and money. We roomed together at school, you see, and she used to help me with my Spanish—that Spanish that you say is just 'adequate'—and I helped her to polish her English. She speaks perfectly but she wanted to sound more colloquial."

César smiled. It lit up his face and made him seem younger than the touch of gray at his temples would suggest. "I see you are not one to forget insults. But really, your Spanish is quite good, though perhaps a little stiff. This visit should remedy that, if you're staying very long at all."

Catherine shook her head. "I'm a working girl, a poor schoolteacher. I'm just taking part of our long Christmas holiday for this visit. It's a good break from the winter weather at home, and María Lucía wanted me to come during the sugar cane festival. She says there are lots of parties and public events then."

"Yes, you've come at the right time to the right place," he rejoined. "Besides, it is said that the people of Cali—the *caleños*—speak the nearest thing in the world today to the beautiful Spanish of Spain's Golden Age, because we are in the interior and thus isolated from many corrupting influences, such as English."

Catherine raised her eyebrows. "That sounds rather conservative, as if you weren't in favor of progress. The world is becoming one big family; someday we will all have one skin and one language."

"Hah!" don César exploded. "To preserve one's culture is a duty. The Mexicans no longer speak the language of their forefathers. They wear cheap imitations of American dress—"

"One doesn't think about preserving Culture with a

9

capital *C* when one has to make a living," Catherine broke in. "It's all most people can do to deal with the basic problems of food, clothing, and shelter."

"And you, Catherine Gray, do you have a culture worth preserving, worth fighting for? Or do Leonardo and I have a little revolutionary on our hands?" César asked with a touch of sarcasm. He leaned toward her, almost touching her knee, and looked as if he were controlling a rising anger. Catherine felt at once frightened and thrilled by his nearness.

"I don't suppose I do," she said, trying to calm the tremors of excitement in her bones. "I come from a long line of simple people, mostly farmers and country schoolteachers. My parents have a small farm that just pays for itself and they certainly don't have any time left at the end of the day for the luxuries, even if they could afford them. They sent me away to school, to make something of myself. I was the hope of the family, I guess you'd say, since I was the only child."

"I see," César said pensively. He sat back abruptly and soon seemed lost in thought. Once Catherine ventured to disturb him by asking, "What do you do for a living? I told you about myself, so now you can tell me," but he only said dryly, "You are too direct. It is best to learn right now that one doesn't ask those questions here." After that, Catherine turned to the window and tried to recognize something of the descriptions María Lucía had told or written her over the years. The big car swooped like an eagle around taxicabs of ancient vintage and crazy old trucks crammed with people and animals. On either side of the roadway stretched fields of sugar cane, occasionally accented by brilliant tropical flowers. The airport was far outside the city, which they were just approaching across the flat valley floor.

Cali, she remembered, was set in the rich Cauca

River Valley, three thousand feet above sea level in the Andes Mountains and three degrees above the equator. Although the eastern slopes of the wide valley were lost in low clouds and mist, Catherine could see the white city climbing the side of the western range. When they were nearer, she could make out one peak crowned by three white crosses and, to its left, another topped by a massive statue with its arms outstretched over the valley. The two summits stood in lonely splendor against the sky, guardians of the city.

Catherine looked longingly at the shimmering buildings, wondering what they held for her. Somehow she had hoped the trip would be a new beginning, or at least provide a salve for her wounds. In spite of it all, however, she must write Alex and let him know she had arrived safely; he would worry. Confused by fatigue, she asked herself why she had argued with César in such a way, making herself sound like a person with no interest in the finer things of life. He would probably mark her down as a typical, unsympathetic tourist. Something about the man antagonized her and yet, she realized with surprise, she wanted him to think well of her.

"Catherine Gray of the gray eyes." He had turned toward her again, smiling, and seemed to have forgotten his annoyance. "Where did you get those marvelous eyes?"

"I—I don't know," Catherine stammered and looked down, as if to hide them from his scrutiny.

"But really, they are remarkable," he pressed. "Did no one ever tell you that you have a striking appearance?"

"No," Catherine said honestly. "I used to be called the Colt when I was growing up, because I was so awkward."

"I imagine you've improved since then." He ap-

11

praised her coolly. "But it is amazing that no one has noticed those eyes, and the way your dark hair sets off your fair skin—"

"Please!"

"—which blushes so nicely."

"I'm an awful sight now," Catherine said lamely. She wished he wouldn't look at her like that, as if she were something in a shop window that he was thinking of buying. She had always thought of herself as a pleasant person to look at, but not naturally beautiful or glamorous in style.

"Yes, a bit bedraggled," César was agreeing, "but you have good bones. If one has good bones, one has possibilities."

"Señor Saavedra," Catherine said with deadly serenity, "where did you get your marvelous arrogance?"

There was a stunned silence in the car. The chauffeur turned to glance at her, as if he had understood what she said and couldn't believe it. César sat motionless, with the look of a man who had just been slapped. Suddenly he threw back his handsome head and laughed heartily.

"So! My prisoner fights back!"

"I'm not your prisoner," Catherine protested, beginning to be alarmed. "You've been very kind, but I could just as well get out here and get a taxi the rest of the way."

"If I were you, I wouldn't try it. Look around you. In this section of the city you would lose more than your precious suitcase if you wandered about alone."

They had turned into a deeply rutted, unpaved street and were bumping between two long rows of decaying hovels, which seemed to have been built of packing boxes and scraps of tin. Here and there, from an evilly low and dark interior, a half-naked child gazed out hopelessly. Catherine caught her breath as a scrawny

12

chicken started up before the onslaught of the Mercedes and grazed the windshield in its frantic flight. She had heard about such slums, but had never imagined they could be so desolate. In a blighted, open space where some of the dwellings had been torn down, she saw several ungainly shapes silhouetted in a tree and realized with horror that they were vultures. She had never seen any before except in pictures and was unpleasantly surprised to find that living creatures could be so revolting. A few blocks farther they crossed what appeared to be a stagnant, foul-smelling creek. "The *aguas negras*," César explained. "Open sewers." Catherine grimaced with distaste.

"Shall we declare a truce? I'm afraid you've been seeing too many films about Latins. We don't really abduct helpless maidens. At least not often," he finished sardonically.

Catherine bit her lip to keep from making a harsh rejoinder and turned away in humiliation. For the rest of the ride she forced herself to observe the city. From the slums they drove through the bustling business section, with its exotic blend of the modern and the primitive, and began a curving ascent of a flank of the western mountain range. The square stone houses of the residential districts fronted directly onto the street, offering only an occasional glimpse through iron grillwork of the flower-hung patios around which the life of the families revolved. At intervals uniformed maids appeared to polish brass door fittings or to sweep a short entrancewalk.

As the city fell away behind them the cooler air revived Catherine and made her eager to see María Lucía and to begin exploring the city. She had not seen her old roommate since school days but a frequent exchange of letters had kept them fast friends. María Lucía had spent many school holidays with Catherine on the farm, since she could not often make the long trip home to Colombia. In spite of her obviously privileged upbringing, her natural kindness and grace had made her a favorite with Catherine's parents, who still chuckled over María Lucía's dainty attempts at pitching hay and milking. Catherine had met María Lucía's father only once, at their graduation, and remembered him vaguely as a courtly but reserved gentleman of advanced years.

Violet Imbert, the mother, had made a more dramatic impression. "My daughter is the real violet of the family," she used to say. "I fear that I am a headier fragrance: jungle gardenia, perhaps." Catherine gathered that Violet had been an adventurous Greenwich Village poetess before her marriage to don Carlos, a sober businessman. She was still a poetess, a member of the colorful intelligentsia of Cali, and was known as something of a wit.

Catherine stole a glance at her companion. He was chatting with the chauffeur about someone named Isabel and appeared elaborately unconcerned with his passenger. He was a rude man, Catherine thought, who had probably offered her a ride with the prospect of idle amusement at her expense. He looked as if he were very much used to having his own way with people. His hand was spread negligently on the seat between them, the fingers long and sensitive, yet promising great strength. She thought of a fist in a velvet glove.

At that moment the car slid to the curb and Catherine looked out at a pleasant stucco building, the arched entranceway of which was framed by twining vines of crimson bougainvillea. As she watched, a curtain twitched upstairs behind an iron-barred window. Catherine scrambled to gather up her shoulder bag and

14

jacket as the chauffeur took her suitcase to the door and handed it to the uniformed maid who answered his ring. He returned and held the car door open for Catherine.

César Saavedra turned easily and took Catherine's hand in his own. Looking straight into her eyes, he said seriously, "It has been my pleasure and my good fortune to welcome you to my country, Catherine Gray. I hope you will not remember it as a bad welcome."

His sincerity disarmed her. "Oh, no, please," she protested, "you mustn't think me ungrateful. I appreciate your kindness very much and I—I'm glad to have met you."

He smiled with just the corners of his mouth. "We are both saying polite words, the ones people are supposed to say at a time like this. I wonder if these polite words really mean anything, however."

Catherine smiled in return, but unsurely. "I don't know what you mean." Since he did not reply, she said awkwardly, "Happy New Year." Wordlessly he released her hand and she got out and let herself be escorted to the door by Leonardo. Once she looked back and felt a wave of weakness break over her at the sight of him sitting back against the cushions, his head turned slightly to look at her. There was no doubt about it, he was a very attractive man. Then she heard a familiar voice squeal, "Oh, Catherine, I'm so glad you're here!" and was caught up in the welcoming arms of María Lucía.

"You haven't changed a bit!" Catherine exclaimed warmly, holding her friend at arm's length. María Lucía, short and vivacious with a slight tendency to plumpness, wore a ruffled dress of heliotrope lawn that set her pleasantly rounded features aglow.

"You look wonderful, Catherine, very professional," María Lucía responded.

"Professional? What do you mean by that?" Catherine asked, nonplussed. "It sounds rather unfeminine."

"Oh, darling, I just mean that I can imagine you in that suit, standing before your class and saying very learned things."

"Oh dear," sighed Catherine, feeling ungainly and drab beside the Latin sparkle of María Lucía, as she often had at school. "But what about you? You have a job and have to be professional, too, don't you?"

"Oh, my job at the tourist agency isn't very serious." She giggled. "It's just something to do until I find someone to marry. See? I took the whole day off because you were coming."

"Catherine, my dear!" Violet Imbert, in a trailing turquoise caftan, descended the curved, wrought-iron staircase and swept toward them. She embraced Catherine and kissed her solemnly on the forehead, as if to place a seal upon the occasion. Then she stepped back and dropped her imposing manner as quickly as she had assumed it. "Tell me right now, before María Lucía and I die of curiosity," she said, smiling impishly, "how on God's green earth you managed to get hold of César Saavedra on your very first day in Colombia."

"Oh, why? Is he somebody?" Catherine asked innocently.

"Is he somebody!" Violet exclaimed. "Is a bluebird blue? But we forget ourselves. Dear, show Catherine where she can freshen up. Then we'll discuss this exciting development over a nice cup of Colombian coffee."

Twenty minutes later, much refreshed by a quick shower and a change into a pale yellow shirt and skirt, Catherine joined the two women in a sunny room overlooking the patio. Screened on three sides, the room was furnished with bright-cushioned wicker furniture and hanging baskets of ferns. In one corner an ornate

16

brass bird cage swung gently with the movement of its chirping inhabitants.

Catherine looked down into the patio, where orchids spilled out of niches in the high, whitewashed walls, and let out a long, satisfied sigh. "This is so beautiful. How could you endure our bare, cold dormitory rooms, María Lucía, when you had this to think about?"

"Perhaps they were as exotic to me as this is to you," María Lucía smiled. "Tell me, how are your parents?"

"They're fine, still working as hard as ever," Catherine answered. She felt a lump in her throat as she recalled how she had defended them to César Saavedra. A man like that would probably never understand the worth of good, honest working people.

Having poured the rich, aromatic coffee into demitasse cups, Violet offered a plate of cookies and jellied guava squares. "I'm glad you had the experience of meeting César Saavedra, Catherine," she began, "but since you're only staying such a short while anyway, why couldn't it have been María Lucía! We could do with an introduction to someone like that, couldn't we, *mija*?"

María Lucía raised her eyes heavenward in mock ecstasy. "Oh, Catherine, how did you manage it? Didn't he tell you anything about himself? The Saavedras are one of the oldest and most influential families in the country. It is even said that a Saavedra was in the group of Spaniards who founded Cali in 1536. They are true aristocrats and practically unapproachable by all but their own kind. They live in a world apart. Don César has vast holdings in sugar cane and coffee. The family hacienda, Los Limonares, is said to be the oldest and largest in the valley and its history is intertwined with the history of Colombia. Even the great Simón Bolívar visited there."

17

"So you know his family?" Catherine asked hopefully. The thought of never seeing César again was curiously depressing.

"No, we don't know them," Violet explained, "although everyone knows of them. You see, in Latin America there still exists a kind of class system. It is based on wealth, but not only on wealth. We are new money, he is old money, and seldom the twain do meet. Of course my status as a writer has enabled me to range rather more freely than most among the social classes and I have had some opportunity to observe the upper crust. Let me tell you, it is true that the rich are different from you and me: they have a kind of *noblesse oblige* that makes them behave in a special way."

"I suppose, then, that he was obliged to help me, a damsel in distress," laughed Catherine. "I lost a suitcase and didn't have a ride here from the airport. But just imagine a man like that having the nerve to tell me not to care about possessions! Anyway, we didn't exactly hit it off. I told him he was arrogant."

"You didn't!" cried María Lucía. "No one talks to the Saavedras like that!"

"Well, he is," said Catherine defensively. "And I have a feeling that I spoke out against the very values he cherishes, such as the importance of tradition."

Violet shook her head regretfully. "Well, my dear, you can take comfort from the fact that it probably would have come to nothing anyway. But I'm afraid you've made the worse possible impression."

"I guess you're right," Catherine was forced to agree. "But tell me one more thing, something I was curious about. Do you know how he came by the scar on his cheek? It's quite dashing."

"Oh, yes," Violet nodded. "It is not an easy thing to be wealthy here. Some years ago there was a kidnaping attempt on the road to Los Limonares. César escaped with that scar. He fought like a tiger, I understand, and only one of the ruffians got away. No, his life has not been a happy one, I think. There were other things. . . ." She trailed off as a maid came in to remove the coffee service, and when conversation recommenced, it was about the plans made for Catherine's visit.

That evening María Lucía's brother Eduardo, a successful lawyer, brought their aunt and uncle to dinner, making a full family assemblage in honor of Catherine's arrival; but by the time the meal was over, Catherine begged to be excused early and went to her room, with the sympathy of her hosts. So many new impressions crowding upon her had brought her to a state of giddy exhaustion and she yearned for rest. Yet, as she was getting ready for bed, she paused before the mirror of her dressing table and studied her reflection closely. Were her eyes really marvelous? Alex had always told her she was pretty, but she had assumed he was merely being kind.

She lifted her thick, dark hair and let it fall back around her shoulders, studying the effect. Perhaps she could be genuinely attractive if she tried. Her features were regular enough and her figure quite presentable. True, she seldom had time to think much about her appearance. It was always a lick and a promise as she hurried off to a meeting or to school, telling herself that on the weekend she would shop for a new dress or get her hair done. But weekends were even busier with chores like weeding the kitchen garden or canning, so she never did. Again she heard the mellow, slightly accented voice say, "If one has good bones, one has possibilities." But it was no use thinking about him. Violet Imbert had made it abundantly clear that he belonged to a world that would never open its doors to a country-bred schoolteacher. *Yet even a cat may look at a king,* thought Catherine wistfully as she climbed into bed and stretched gratefully between the cool sheets. She was fast asleep when, some time later, there was a knock at the door and the maid brought in her lost suitcase, which bore a card reading, "With the compliments of César Saavedra Solano."

CHAPTER TWO

A tolling bell woke Catherine the next morning just after dawn. Although the upstairs of the house was still quiet, from downstairs rose the bustle of the maids in the kitchen and the intoxicating smell of Colombian coffee. Slipping on her robe, Catherine went to the window. Her room was in the front of the house; it overlooked the street and faced the western mountains. To her left she could see the range called the Farallones. From her talks with María Lucía, who had often been homesick at school, she remembered that the Farallones were generally hidden in the clouds; but this morning they stood out against a clear blue sky, the rays of the rising sun sheathing their ordinarily somber slopes in cloth of gold. They were showing themselves as a welcome to her, Catherine decided. She would take their appearance as a good omen.

Opening the French windows inward, she leaned on the wide sill and looked out past the bars. A ragged boy trundled a pushcart heaped with oranges down the street, calling out in a nasal singsong. Further on, a uniformed policeman in front of one of the foreign em-

21

bassies stifled a yawn and continued pacing in front of the fence. From somewhere came the raucous cry of a parrot. Catherine watched as the Imberts' cook came out with a large basket and hailed the boy with the oranges. She had not felt so alive in years as she did just then, quietly taking in the morning sights and sounds. Perhaps it was the exciting unfamiliarity of her surroundings; or perhaps her mother was right when she had said that Catherine was too responsible and ought to let herself have more fun. It was so easy to let life pass you by, her mother had said, and Catherine had been afraid to ask if her mother had wanted something more than the safe, rural existence into which she had settled so young.

At seven there was a knock at the door and a maid came in with a tray of hot rolls, juice, and coffee. In answer to Catherine's questions, she confirmed that the juice had been freshly made from oranges bought that morning and that the Señora Violet had already breakfasted in her room, as usual, and would spend most of the morning writing. Catherine ate at a little table by the window and was just finishing when María Lucía stuck her head in the door.

"Good morning! I hope you slept enough? Things start moving so early in this household."

"Yes, I did, thank you, and I feel human again." Catherine pushed away the remains of her breakfast. "I was just at the window, watching the street wake up. What is the bell I heard?"

"It is the bell of the orphanage. You can see the bell tower from the other side of the house, and often the tiny outline of the boy who rings the bell. My mother belongs to a group of ladies who do charity work and the orphanage is one of their greatest concerns. We may visit it later, if you'd like."

"I would like to see as much as possible," Catherine

said. "Now come in and chat awhile. We have so much catching up to do."

"Yes, letters are a poor substitute for face-to-face talks," María Lucía agreed, taking a seat on the bed. "I'm glad your Alex was willing to share you with us for a little while."

Catherine winced. "I'm afraid he wasn't very willing, María Lucía. We had a dreadful quarrel."

"I hope it was not really serious. Didn't you write to me that you are going to be married?"

Catherine shrugged. "Yes, but now I don't know what will happen. I can't imagine my life without Alex, I suppose, because we've known each other so long and have made so many plans. You remember the picture of him I kept on my bookshelf at school. But when I wanted to make this trip, he became very angry and told me I was selfish. He thought that I should spend the holidays at home with our families, as I always have done, instead of going off to enjoy myself alone."

"He sounds very possessive—maybe like Latin American men?" suggested María Lucía.

"No, Alex is not that way, or he never has been. He just believes that there is a right way and a wrong way to do things. His family is very proper. Now he accuses me of being too 'liberated' and says that a rising merchant's wife—or fiancée—must be aware of her social position, of what people will think."

"It sounds as if he feels unsure of you," commented María Lucía.

"But why should he?" protested Catherine. "I've never given him any cause."

"You didn't cancel your trip," her friend said slyly.

"You know, you're right," Catherine agreed with a frown, "and that's what puzzles me about myself. After we quarreled, I felt as if I were suffocating, as if I

23

needed room to breathe. I really expected that I would back down at the last minute and please Alex by staying home. I'm sure he thought so too. And yet I didn't. Not only that, but when I stepped onto the plane, I felt as if a weight had been lifted from my heart."

"Maybe your heart wanted a holiday."

"But I love Alex!" Catherine exclaimed.

"Sometimes love can become a duty," María Lucía said gently.

"No, no," Catherine insisted. "Alex is very good to me and I'm sure he will be a considerate husband. He's not usually demanding, but I guess my determination to go just surprised him, as it surprised me. We'll patch it up, I'm sure."

"It's just as well to have a good quarrel before you're married," María Lucía said helpfully. "That way you resolve questions that might be a problem later."

"Yes, let's look on the bright side," said Catherine. "But tell me something. What you said about Latin American men being possessive—how true is that? I've heard they're very jealous."

María Lucía nodded. "Oh, yes, I'd say most of the stories are true. You see, I am especially aware of it because I have a foot in two worlds. I grew up here in Colombia, but my mother took care to send me to the States at times, so that I would experience both cultures. I would have more independence if I married an American or Englishman, but the Latin American life is very tempting also. The men here, they make you feel very special and secure, as if you are a china figurine that must be carefully protected. But," she cautioned, "don't get involved with anyone in Colombia unless you are ready to belong to him heart and soul."

"Heart and soul," Catherine repeated thoughtfully as she idly twisted a lock of hair. After a moment she rose and went to the closet to pick out her clothes for the day, remarking, "I hardly think there's any likelihood of my becoming involved with a man here. Besides, I didn't come for that."

"No, of course not." Her friend smiled. "But this is an exciting country, a place where the unexpected often happens. And tonight you'll have a chance to meet some interesting people. That's really what I came in to tell you. I forgot to mention yesterday that we're giving a party in your honor tonight. No, now don't protest! My circle of friends includes both Colombians and members of the foreign community, so I invited some of each. There will be dancing, typical foods, and probably guitar-playing and singing toward the end."

"You're so good to me," Catherine said. "I'm not used to such attention."

"My mother and I want this visit to be something you will remember the rest of your life," María Lucía said warmly.

As the day passed and Catherine began to accustom herself to the leisurely pace of life in Cali, she told herself more than once that she could never forget her South American vacation. In fact, she was already looking ahead with regret to the time, just a few days hence, when it would be only a happy memory. She would go back to finish the school year and then, in early summer, she and Alex would finally be married. They had prudently agreed to put off marriage until his promotion to assistant manager of the store came through, which it had, just before Christmas. In the fall she would go back to teaching and would continue to do so until the children came—2.4 of them, Alex joked; they might as well conform to the national average. More than likely, they would continue to live in the same town, unless Alex went into business for himself in a larger population center. She could see him doing that, for he was progressive in his ideas and hard-working. They would have a good life and she was lucky to have such a comfortable future ahead of her. Many girls would envy her, in fact. But it would not be, Catherine reflected, a life in which the unexpected often happened.

At lunchtime Violet Imbert emerged exhausted from her bedroom-study, declaring that the muse of poetry had flown out the window and was perched in a chestnut tree down the street, leaving her only a few miserable lines of verse for the morning's work. Since María Lucía had gone downtown to her job. Violet promised that after a siesta she would take Catherine out to see a bit of the city.

"The best way to get the flavor of a place is simply to follow a native around on his errands," Violet asserted as they stepped into a taxi some hours later. Catherine soon saw her point. There seemed to be a thousand small things that had to be ferreted out one by one in small shops all over the city, with much negotiating and gesturing. At last, flushed with the heat of the afternoon, they stopped in a café for coffee.

"Running a household down here is like being general of an army," Violet told Catherine. "There are few department stores and labor-saving devices. You see how many things I have to attend to personally."

"I'm amazed," said Catherine. "One has to know about so many different things."

"It took me long enough to learn, I can tell you that. Carlos was very patient with me in the beginning, when I would overspend the housekeeping budget or fail at finding the right repairman. But in twenty-five years I have never for one second been bored. I wonder how many people can say that." Catherine agreed it was something to consider.

As they were finishing their coffee Violet suddenly

said, "By the way, the maid told me that your suitcase came last night."

Catherine was annoyed to feel her cheeks growing hot. "Yes, it was sent by, you know, that gentleman, César Saavedra."

"Lord knows how he ran it down, but I suppose a man like that has connections everywhere." Violet's eyes narrowed pensively. "It's quite interesting. Frankly, I'm surprised he went to the trouble."

"I'm sure anyone would have done the same," Catherine said.

"No," Violet shook her head, "I don't think so. You mark my words. You'll be hearing from him again."

"Will we be going by the post office? I have a letter to mail to Alex," Catherine said too severely, willing herself to change the subject. She refused to spend one more minute with that dark, distant face swimming before her eyes.

For the party that evening Catherine chose a rustling black taffeta skirt and a high-necked, lace-trimmed blouse of fine batiste. The blouse had cost too much, but it was worth it for the way it felt on her skin. She pulled her hair back in a loose bun, leaving some wisps curling around her face, and added her grandmother's garnet earrings for a spot of color. They were the only heirloom she had and she wore them when she needed to give herself a little confidence. As she dabbed perfume behind her ears, she heard the first guests arriving downstairs and experienced a thrill of panic. Dainty footsteps came tapping up the stairs and María Lucía tripped into the room. "Come down, Catherine," she begged. "Everyone is dying to meet you. I've told them so much about you."

"Oh, no," Catherine wailed, "you shouldn't have. I mean, there's nothing special about meeting me. I—I'll be down in a minute. I have to—"

"Nonsense," María Lucía interrupted, taking her friend by the arm. Catherine's heart sank farther with each step down the staircase. She had always been somewhat shy and unsure of herself in public, but the prospect of an entire group of strangers waiting to meet her completely unnerved her. Although she had been rather pleased with her appearance a few moments earlier, by comparison with María Lucía she must look absolutely spinsterish, she concluded. Her friend wore high-heeled gold sandals and a full-skirted, filmy dress in riotous colors. Whereas Catherine had used just a touch of lipstick and mascara, María Lucía's face was made radiant by an expert application of eye shadows, blushers, and powders.

Somehow Catherine managed to greet the first arrivals and make enough conversation so that she was not left standing alone, as she had feared. María Lucía's friends were very attentive and when the dancing started, Señor Imbert took her out on the floor and taught her the stately two-step called the *pasodoble*. She began to relax a little and was deep in a conversation about flowers with a neighbor of the Imberts' when María Lucía brought a latecomer over to be introduced.

"Catherine, this is Frank Gibson. He's living proof that when Colombia gets in your blood, it's hard to get away again."

Frank Gibson grinned and took Catherine's hand. Immediately she liked him for his firm handshake and honest, open countenance. "That's right," he agreed. "What about you? Down here for long?"

"No, just a short visit, I'm afraid."

"Oh, sure, María Lucía told me," Frank Gibson remembered. "But then you never know. I came down for a two-year stint with the Peace Corps and here I still am."

28

María Lucía was called away and Catherine found herself alone with her new acquaintance. He was tall and muscular, with crackling blue eyes and an unruly shock of wheat-colored hair. His eyebrows had been bleached nearly white by the southern sun, so that his unusually blue eyes were made even more prominent. All in all, however, he made Catherine think of a good-humored, golden bear.

"What made you stay?" she wanted to know.

"Well, I was just a kid when I got here," Frank began. "Oh, I thought I was old enough and big enough to change the world. Full of great ideas, you know. I was supposed to give the peasant farmers advice on crop rotation, fertilizers, and the like and for a while I thought I would turn everything around single-handedly and wipe out poverty. You can guess what happened. Not everybody cared to change his living patterns because of what some young foreigner told him. Then, too, I didn't know as much as I thought I did. There were problems with equipment and bureaucratic foul-ups. I've never worked so hard in my life to accomplish so little. Not that I'm afraid of hard work, you understand. But this place got under my skin. I liked the people and I liked the land. When my stint in the Corps was up, I decided that since I had no ties to speak of back home, I'd stay and make a life for myself here. After a while it was too late to go back; that is, I don't think I'd fit anymore."

"Are you sorry now?" Catherine asked.

"No, but I guess a lot of people would say I'm a fool. It's not a bed of roses, not as comfortable as I would have it back home. Maybe it's the challenge that attracts me."

"What do you do for a living?" Catherine inquired.

Frank Gibson hesitated. "Look, I don't want to monopolize your time. I don't see too many people these

29

days and when I find somebody who will listen, I'm liable to talk his ear off. Maybe you don't know anything about farming, anyway."

"Oh, but I do. I was born on one." Catherine smiled. "Go on. I'll let you know when I get tired."

"Okay, here's the set-up. I bought myself a little farm up on the Carretera al Mar, that is, the Road to the Sea. A lot of it is hillside and not arable, but it sure is pretty. There's a flat part about halfway down where I raise cattle. I have a worker who lives in a little cabin down there and he and his wife do the milking and make cheese. The main house, where I live, is up next to the road. It's your typical Colombian farmhouse, with a red tile roof and a porch around three sides. I put a picture window in the other wall, which looks out over the valley. I could sit there by the hour and watch the storms come and go, the fog settle down, the sunset, the stars. It's better than a picture show. On the slopes near the house we raise food for ourselves, plus some things for market, like pineapple and yucca. I've been experimenting with what might be considered delicacies for the foreign community, too, such as broccoli and strawberries. The soil isn't as rich as it is down in the valley, but I do pretty well. And I still share whatever expertise I have when people come to me for help." Frank Gibson's eyes shone as he talked, and Catherine's heart went out to him in his enthusiasm. He was so easy to talk to that she found all her nervousness had dissipated.

"How do you happen to know María Lucía?" she asked.

"Mutual friends," he replied. "But I work too hard now to be on the party circuit, so I don't see as many people as I used to. Say, if you don't mind dancing with an old farmer, let's give it a whirl. Who knows when I'll have another chance to take a pretty girl in my arms."

Violet had had the Ecuadorian rugs removed from the living room and the smooth stone floor was crowded with dancers. Catherine let Frank lead her through the crush until they found a vacant space. When he took her in his arms, she felt the brute strength of the man. Frank Gibson was not exactly a graceful dancer but he was steady and sure in his lead, so that she was able to forget her own lack of practice and let herself be carried along. When the record had finished, he released her but made no move to leave the floor. The next song was another slow one, which they managed with a box step, but the tempo picked up after that. They stopped to watch the other dancers flying through a series of intricate steps that expressed the Latin rhythms perfectly.

"That's too many for me," Frank laughed. "Why don't we sit this one out?" They found seats in the patio, where tables had been set up around the goldfish pool. Frank brought two cups of punch and a plate of sandwiches.

"Are the nights always so beautiful here?" Catherine breathed. "The air is so . . . heady, somehow. It makes me feel like singing."

"This city air is nothing," Frank declared. "Wait till you see how it is up at my place. It's cooler up there. A few lungfuls of that good mountain air would cure any ailment." He stopped at the surprised look on Catherine's face and stammered, "Oh, I'm sorry. I got ahead of myself, I guess, and leaped to conclusions. I just thought I could help you to see a little more of Colombia, if you'd like. My farm is about half an hour from here. If you're not doing anything else, you and María Lucía could come up on Sunday morning and spend the day. If you come early enough, we could go to the open-air market at Kilometer Thirty. That's something the ordinary tourist doesn't see. How about it?"

"I'd love to," Catherine said, "that is, if María Lucía agrees. Is it hard to find?"

"Oh, no," Frank assured her. "Anyway, María Lucía's been up before."

Catherine had been so engrossed in Frank Gibson's attentions that she had lost track of her friend in the throng of guests. As Frank talked on about his plans for the farm and his experiences as a foreigner in South America, she began to look around. At last she saw María Lucía glance down from the fern room, where she was chatting with a young doctor from the hospital. Catherine waved to catch her attention. As their eyes met, María Lucía looked from Catherine to Frank and raised her eyebrows. *Come down here,* Catherine mouthed.

Moments later María Lucía slid gracefully into the chair beside them and Catherine explained, "Frank has been telling me all about his farming adventure up on the Carretera al Mar and he's invited us to come up for the whole day on Sunday. Do you think we could do it? I'd be interested in seeing a working farm here, you know, and it would be something to tell my parents about."

It seemed to Catherine that María Lucía's smile was a bit too bright and wide. "That's very generous of you, Frank," she said carefully. "I'm sure it can be arranged. We'll bring a picnic."

"Afraid to trust my cooking?" Frank teased. "But look, if you're bringing food, could you ask your cook to include some of those ginger cookies she makes? They're the best I've ever tasted."

"Of course," María Lucía said politely as she nervously twisted her bangle bracelets.

Catherine stood up. "If you two will excuse me for a minute, I think I'll go to my room for a shawl. It's a little cooler than I thought and I'd hate to catch a chill at the beginning of my visit." She walked casually away, then, once out of sight, quickened her pace and soon was shutting her bedroom door behind her. She slipped off her shoes and sat down on the bed to think. It occurred to her that ever since her arrival, she had only been talking about herself. And Alex used to say she was so retiring! She had not asked María Lucía about her own social life and now it seemed strange that her friend, usually so confiding, had not volunteered any information.

There was no mistaking María Lucía's discomfort in the presence of Frank Gibson. It was possible that when she and Frank had been talking in the patio, María Lucía had been watching them—spying?—from the fern room. But why? Frank Gibson had seemed at ease. After all, he had invited both of them to the farm. Perhaps, Catherine puzzled, María Lucía felt she was only being asked out of courtesy and was jealous of Catherine's invitation. Yet Frank seemed familiar with the cooking of the Imbert household and María Lucía had visited his farm before. Could it be, Catherine wondered, that María Lucía was harboring a secret affection for Frank? That would explain her barely concealed anguish and his unconcern. Catherine looked at the clock on the dresser and calculated that she had probably spent two hours in his company. How wounding that would have been to María Lucía, watching helplessly. Catherine determined to go to María Lucía and discover the truth of the situation. If her friend was in love with Frank, she would not stand in her way. On the other hand, she thought, a smile tugging at the corners of her mouth, if Frank was free of claims, open or secret, she wouldn't mind getting to know him better. He was fun.

As Catherine descended the stairs again, she saw that the party was still in full swing. Someone had turned off the record player and two guitarists were singing Latin American folk songs to a cluster of guests. The maids plied back and forth from the kitchen, bringing fresh pitchers of punch and trays of hot appetizers. Catherine looked down into the patio, but the table where she had left Frank and María Lucía had been taken by another couple. She circulated through the downstairs rooms, smiling at new acquaintances and trying to catch sight of either Frank or María Lucía. Neither was anywhere to be found. She had just decided to look upstairs when she heard her name called and turned to find Violet Imbert, in another flowing gown, bearing down upon her.

"Catherine, dear! I've been looking everywhere for you. Can you imagine what this is?" She waved a thick, cream-colored envelope dramatically.

"No, I've no idea," Catherine said.

"I'll bet I know," Violet declared triumphantly. "What do you bet? It just came by messenger and was brought to me by the maid, but I'm sure I know who sent it. Here."

Catherine's mouth felt dry as she took the envelope from Violet and fumbled it open. The first time she read the words, they did not register. Then the bold, black scrawl began to arrange itself into meaning. She looked up at Violet, her eyes wide. "It's . . . he . . ." she said faintly, "he'll . . . be here at ten tomorrow. He wants to show me the city."

"Is it who I think it is?" Violet demanded.

"Yes. I suppose. It's from César Saavedra."

On impulse Violet hugged Catherine. "Congratulations! If nothing else, it will make a good story to tell your grandchildren."

Catherine struggled to appear unconcerned. She hoped Violet would not notice how the envelope shook in her hand. Taking a deep breath, she said, "I wonder if you know where María Lucía is. I can't seem to find her."

"I think she's in the kitchen. Come on, let's tell her your good news," Violet suggested, herding Catherine before her.

One look at María Lucía's face assured Catherine that her suspicions were correct. The girl was listlessly supervising the cook and scarcely managed a smile when the other two came in.

"Such thrilling developments," caroled Violet. "Catherine is to be squired about the city tomorrow by Señor Saavedra."

"Really?" her daughter said without much interest.

"María Lucía," Catherine said quickly, "let me help you in here for a while. I'm a little tired of being a social butterfly." As soon as Violet quit fussing around the stove and went off to see to the other guests, Catherine went on, "It was very nice of your friend Frank Gibson to invite us to his farm. He must be a very good friend to do that—I mean, to help you entertain me."

"He's not doing it for me," María Lucía returned coldly.

Catherine feigned disbelief. "Why, what do you mean? He's giving you a hand at entertaining your guest. Very considerate of him, I'd say."

María Lucía turned from the stove and patted Catherine's arm. "Nice try, Catherine, but it won't work. Frank has taken a liking to you and he wants to see more of you, that's all. Go and enjoy yourself."

"You mean go by myself? I will not! But please tell

me what there is between you two," Catherine pleaded. "The last thing in the world I want to do is make you unhappy."

María Lucía measured Catherine with a long look, then broke into a rueful smile. "I know that," she said sincerely, "but you needn't worry. This is how it was. About a year ago Frank and I met at a party not unlike this one. We seemed to have a lot in common, that is, general things like our senses of humor and certain values. We saw each other constantly for about three months, until my family stepped in. They have rather old-fashioned ideas about love and marriage, for all my mother's bohemian youth. You'd think that at least my brother would understand, but he's the worst one. Anyway, they thought I was wasting my time with Frank. Since he is fairly poor and has no social standing, he would make an unsuitable partner down here. Finally they insisted that I stop seeing him alone, although as you can see, he's still welcome in the house as a friend."

"But what about Frank himself, didn't he object?" Catherine wondered.

"Frank is proud," María Lucía sighed. "At first he was insulted and I didn't know what he might do. But later he said something about 'When in Rome, do as the Romans do' and stopped calling. I couldn't understand it. I thought he would be more stubborn than that. I didn't see anything of him until recently, and I just invited him tonight to show him there were no hard feelings. Looking back, I can see that the whole thing must have been my fault. He wasn't as serious as I was. If he had been, he would have defied my family. To him, I was just another girl. I want you to go and have fun, but I'm not ready yet to pretend that nothing happened and be merely a friend to him."

"I wouldn't like to go under these circumstances,"

Catherine said, "although my commitment to Alex should put you at ease. Let's talk about it tomorrow."

María Lucía and the cook finished draining the oil from a succulent mound of fried plantain chips and Catherine offered to take them in to the buffet table. She came upon Frank Gibson as she was crossing the entrance hall.

"Say, I've been looking for you," he said. To Catherine's great surprise, he gripped her free wrist and said in an intimate whisper, "You won't let me down, now? I'm really looking forward to seeing you up at my place Sunday. I'm leaving now."

Catherine pulled her wrist away and replied frostily, "Yes, of course. It was so kind of you to invite the two of us." She was glad to see that he gave her a puzzled look as he ducked out the door. That would teach him. She certainly had no intention of coming between María Lucía and Frank, even if he seemed to feel perfectly free. Why had he taken hold of her like that? Catherine was a private person and disliked being touched by strangers. She had liked him on impulse, and it was on impulse that she had agreed to visit his farm, but she was beginning to like the idea less and less. She decided that she must be careful and not let the unfamiliar environment throw her off balance, causing her to make mistakes in judgment about people.

After the party was over, Catherine sat on her bed, too keyed up to sleep. She was glad she did not live in a society that separated the social classes so strictly. Poor María Lucía might end up in an arranged marriage, enviable on the outside but empty within. Catherine had always believed that one should be able to follow one's heart, wherever it might lead. She asked herself where her heart was leading her. Just then it felt curiously still, as if it did not know which direction

37

to take. It occurred to her that she ought to write a letter to Alex, with whom she was so used to sharing every crumb of her experiences. Since she had set foot in Colombia, it seemed that things were happening to her so fast that he would never catch up.

But what would she tell him? *Alex, tomorrow I am going on a tour of Cali with a member of the landed aristocracy. He's exciting, a beautiful man. The next day I'll spend with a free spirit in the mountains. He's exciting and beautiful, too, though in a different way. This is all happening to your Catherine, whom you used to call Miss Mousie.* A pang of guilt struck Catherine as she realized that she either should not write Alex at all or she should leave out most of what was befalling her. If she told the truth, he would either be enraged or deeply hurt. His objections to the trip would prove true, in a sense.

And yet an even more troublesome thought began to dawn on her. For years she had been content, even proud, to see herself through Alex's eyes. Alex had been her mirror and he had led her to believe that she was pretty enough and smart enough in a quiet sort of way. There was something rather patronizing in the moderate way he admired her, as if she should be grateful that he, Alex Hampton, found her pleasing. *Perhaps I would be beautiful if someone I loved really believed I was beautiful,* thought Catherine. *Perhaps I could be uniquely intelligent and caring if someone saw that in me.* Again she reached out and took the envelope from her night table. The card inside read; "Little Colt, it would give me great pleasure to introduce you to this city. I will call for you at ten tomorrow. César Saavedra Solano."

Catherine weighed the heavy sheet between her fingertips. She must assume that his intentions were only to show hospitality, in spite of the familiarity of the salutation. After all, his social position was surely under more constraints than María Lucía's. Her head still whirling with possibilities and unanswered questions, Catherine turned out the light and lay down. Before she fell asleep, she promised herself that by tomorrow evening she would have seen César Saavedra for the last time. That would be better for everyone.

CHAPTER THREE

"Catherine? Catherine! Wake up, it's nine thirty!"

Catherine threw back the covers and stumbled to the door to admit María Lucía.

"Oh no," she groaned, "I'll never be ready by ten, and I was determined to look nice today. Of all the luck!"

María Lucía, in a dressing gown, carried in a tray and set it on the foot of the bed. "I brought you a cup of coffee," she said. "Mother forgot you were going out this morning and gave instructions to the maids to let us sleep as long as we wanted. The doorbell woke me—there's a special delivery letter for you."

"Slip it inside my purse, will you?" cried Catherine as she scooped up an armful of clothes and dashed for the shower.

At precisely ten o'clock, as Catherine was hurriedly smoothing her stockings and giving a final flip of the hairbrush to her curls, the big Mercedes came to a halt below her windows and she saw the chauffeur, Leonardo, step out. He was alone.

"Now why do you suppose César couldn't come for

me himself?" she demanded of María Lucía, who was drinking the untouched cup of coffee she had brought for Catherine.

"Good heavens, Catherine, isn't it enough that he sent the car? You should be impressed."

"Well, he needn't be so high and mighty with me. I'm not easily awed," Catherine retorted, much more bravely than she felt. She skimmed down the stairs and soon found herself cradled in the big automobile, progressing through midmorning traffic toward the center of town. It was then, as she reached into her handbag for a mirror, that she saw the letter that had come that morning. She opened it and read in Alex's neat, schoolboy hand:

Dearest Catherine,

Only an hour ago we said good-bye. Don't worry, dear girl, if I said some harsh things. I see now you just want to have your little fling before you settle down to be mine forever. You know I don't approve but I will try to understand just this once! Things are very busy at the store. I just found out that Mr. Manning is leaving me in charge next week while he is out of town. This is my chance to make a good impression. I plan to go by your parents' house tonight and see if they need anything. Be careful you don't get a bad sunburn down there, as I understand the sun is hotter near the equator. And don't forget Your Alex.

Dear Alex, holding the fort, thought Catherine. What would he think if he could see her now! Her stomach was fluttering like a net full of butterflies, though whether it was due to hunger, Alex's letter, or her approaching appointment, she could not say. In another few minutes, however, when Leonardo maneuvered the car to a stop in front of a large building bearing the name Banco de la República, Catherine's heart gave a wild leap. A group of distinguished-looking gentlemen were lingering and talking outside the entrance, as if they had just finished a meeting inside. Standing with his back to her, in a white linen suit, was César Saavedra. He turned slightly, nodded to Leonardo, and began to shake hands around the group.

"I must apologize for not coming to get you myself, but even in Cali, the most fun-loving of cities, business must come before pleasure," César said, leaning in the window. "But now I am free for a few hours. Shall we walk for a while? Leonardo can meet us later.

"This is a novelty for me as well as for you," César went on as they strolled through the crowds. "I seldom come to the city except for business and then I only see the inside of a bank or a lawyer's office."

"You don't live here, then?" Catherine queried.

"I have a house here, yes, but these days I spend most of my time at the hacienda. It is called Los Limonares, for the grove of lemon trees around the house. But what about you? You are enjoying your stay so far? Tell me what you have done."

"I've spent hours talking to María Lucía, catching up on all the news," Catherine answered, "and then there was a party for me last night. Tomorrow I'm invited up to see the farm of a friend of María Lucía's."

"And who is he, this friend?" asked César.

"How did you know it was a he?" Catherine shot back.

"I knew," César replied. "And are you going all alone, Miss Gray, to visit a stranger?"

"I don't know," Catherine said. "That is, María Lucía is invited, too, but for her own reasons she doesn't want to go. I don't quite understand it. Anyway, suppose I am going alone. Why shouldn't I?"

"Why not indeed?" César said agreeably. "You must take advantage of every opportunity in the short time you have here."

Catherine stopped walking and planted her fists on her hips. "Now just a minute. Maybe you have the wrong idea about me, Señor Saavedra. I'm not just looking for people to give me a good time. I accepted Frank Gibson's invitation because it was offered in an impersonal spirit of friendship, for the sake of María Lucía. If a tourist came to see my part of the world, I would do the same for him. But if you think I'm spending the day with him—or you—just to have a story to tell when I get back home, you're very mistaken."

César's eyes sparkled with amusement. "Really, Catherine, I don't think you know what you're talking about. First you say you accepted an invitation because it was offered impersonally. Then in the next breath you seem to say that you do not treat people impersonally. Now try again and tell me exactly what you mean."

"I just mean," Catherine said levelly, "that I am not trying to take advantage of anyone's kindness."

"Now that is something I would like to see," César said dryly. "You trying to take advantage of me."

"Oh!" Catherine stamped her foot. "You're twisting my words!"

"We can't stand on the sidewalk fighting all day. I know a bakery that will have fresh bread coming out of the ovens just about now. Let's take our battle there." He took Catherine's arm and steered her into a side street. Shortly they were met by the moist aroma of rising dough and hot breads. The bakery was on the next corner and had a few small tables alongside heaping

43

bins of baked goods. César seated Catherine and ordered for them both. When the coffee and rolls arrived, Catherine fell on them hungrily. The rolls were piping hot, crunchy with caramelized sugar on top, and buttery inside.

"I like to see a woman who enjoys food," César remarked as he ate at a more leisurely pace. "So many are too concerned with their figures."

Catherine shrugged. "I'm hungry. And these are delicious."

"Did you not have breakfast?"

"No, I didn't have time."

"And why not?"

"Because I didn't want to be late."

"You didn't?"

Catherine set down her cup. "Are you a lawyer, by any chance? You ask so many questions."

César stared at her for what seemed a long time before answering, "If we sat here all day, you would not be able to answer all the questions I have."

The way he was staring at her made Catherine uncomfortable. Later, when she thought back over the day, she decided that if it had not been for that stare, she probably would not have said what she did next. As it was, she blurted, "I'm practically engaged to be married." She looked down as she spoke. When she again looked at César, it seemed to her that a veil of reserve had fallen across his features.

"You know," he said, "you are right about my legal training. I do have a law degree, which I seldom use. And lawyers are interested in the precise meaning of words. So tell me what you mean by 'practically engaged.' "

"I mean that there was no formal announcement of an engagement, but there is a definite agreement. Alex and I have known each other since we were teen-agers. We are planning to be married in the summer."

"In Latin America an engagement is a very serious thing. There is no going back," César commented.

"I suppose it is everywhere," Catherine said in a low voice.

They walked down to the river that bisects the city to see the chapel of La Ermita with its wedding cake ornamentation. On the way back up toward the central square, César remarked on various historical details of the city. Catherine found herself doing the questioning for a change as she asked about the typical handicrafts and finer jewelry and clothing she saw in the shop windows. She reveled in the richness of the street life, in which well-to-do businesspeople, shopgirls in slick copies of the latest fashions, and Indians from the mountains jostled together. Sometimes when she glanced up at César, she thought that his face, with the mouth set in a hard line, looked grimly determined. Other times he appeared relaxed and almost playful. At length they came to the well-known square of Cali, the Plaza Caicedo, a wide space scattered with palm trees and stone benches.

"Are you tired? Leonardo will be waiting for us on the other side," César said.

"I'm fine at the moment," Catherine assured him, "but I'll probably be exhausted tonight, when I stop to think about it."

"Do you know what that little man there is doing, the one with the typewriter?" César asked, pointing to a man in a rusty black suit who was typing on a battered machine as he listened to dictation from an old woman. "He and several others like him are in the plaza every day. If an illiterate peasant needs to have a letter written, he comes to that man and tells him what he wants to say. The man puts the thoughts into very

45

flowery language and types it up for a reasonable fee. He will even write love letters for the tongue-tied, giving expression to thoughts they never had, but which they convince themselves they have after they read what he has typed."

César stopped a few paces from the typist. He glanced slyly at Catherine, then looked off across the plaza, pretending to be deep in thought. "Let me see," he mused. "Suppose I want to have a letter written. I think I will send a letter to a gentleman I have never met. It will begin like this: 'Dear Sir, you are a very fortunate man, so fortunate that I cannot help but wonder if you really realize the extent of your luck. Sometimes when a man discovers buried treasure, he thinks that the discovery is all that counts. He does not realize that that is only the beginning. One must cherish that treasure and husband it carefully or it will be squandered and he will end up poorer than he started, poorer because he had a better chance than most to be rich and he lost it.' " César turned and looked directly into Catherine's eyes as he went on quoting, " 'Now in your case, my dear sir, you did not find buried treasure, but you found something else; you found a Sleeping Beauty. You did not wake her; she is still sleeping. In fact I doubt whether you are capable of waking her. It will take a better man than you—' "

"Stop it!" Catherine cried. "You have no business saying things like that."

César gripped Catherine's arm with steely fingers and began walking again. In a low, resolute voice he said, "Yes, Catherine, you are still sleeping. But the day of your awakening is not so far off as you may think."

Fortunately they had arrived at the car, for Catherine could think of no words with which to reply. She was deeply troubled by the turbulence of her emotions, and furious with César for calling into question everything about her, which he seemed to be doing deliberately. He was playing with her as a cat bats about a mouse.

They drove past parks with spraying fountains, past the bullring and the velodrome and finally out of the city. César was again the perfect guide, directing Leonardo to detour several times so that Catherine could see a wide variety of living conditions. When they passed the university, Catherine asked, "Did you go to school there?"

"No, no, I was educated in Bogotá and abroad because I was expected to handle certain international aspects of the family business," he answered. "My nephew studies there, when he is not too sleepy from staying out all night at discothèques. Someday, I am afraid, there may be no one to take care of things. It is sad when a family comes to an end—" He ceased suddenly, as if he had touched upon a subject too painful to discuss.

Catherine could not keep from asking, "Why don't you like to talk about yourself? You wouldn't really tell me who you were on the way from the airport and now you seem to draw back again. Don't, I'm interested."

She half expected him to turn on her in a rage, but instead he said soberly, "Perhaps it was a release for me to talk to someone who didn't know me. Sometimes I get tired of being who I am. Do you understand that?"

"Yes," Catherine said readily.

"You know, I believe you do, Catherine Gray. I believe you would like to take a vacation from yourself too."

Catherine's eyes widened. "You are the second person to say something like that to me in two days," she marveled, thinking of María Lucía's suggestion that

Catherine's heart wanted a holiday. Was it obvious to everyone but herself?

César was saying, "You see? I know you better than you think. Let me make a suggestion. Let's take a vacation from ourselves together. All right? Then at the end, just like in the fairy tales, we'll change back into our old selves and go our separate ways."

"I'm—I'm not sure what you have in mind," Catherine said uncertainly.

César leaned toward her and asked in a tone of gentle mockery, "What is the matter? Are you afraid of me?" When she did not reply, he added, "Yes, you are afraid of me. But you like it, don't you? You like being afraid."

"I'm not afraid of you!" Catherine protested, but inside she knew he was right. She had never been so deeply afraid.

They had turned off the highway and were traveling in a kind of park. Catherine could see a golf course to one side and, much farther on, tennis courts. "Where are we?" she asked, glad of a chance to change the subject.

"This is a private club," César told her. "What you call a country club, I suppose. I spent a lot of time here as a boy. We can look around and then have lunch."

As they strolled about the grounds, Catherine was once again made aware of the vast gulf between her life and César's. When they looked down on the outdoor pool, César was hailed by several girls who were sunbathing on lawn chairs. It was an elegant, indolent setting, as was the dining room just indoors, where a bridge tournament was in progress. Next they went down to the stables to see the polo ponies and show horses that were being trained there.

"This is not exactly my style of living," Catherine

48

said. "When I was growing up, I swam in a mudhole and rode Sam, my grandfather's mule."

"So we had the same experiences, swimming and riding," César noted with a certain kindness.

"Somehow I think there was a difference," Catherine returned cheerfully.

"Ah, Catherine, I don't know why we came to the stables today. It always makes me sad," he said unexpectedly. He was silent for a while, resting his forearms on the top of a gate and looking out across the fields. Then he said slowly, almost as if he were speaking against his will, "I have a sister named Isabel. She was a beautiful, a radiant, girl, not much younger than you. Three years ago she earned a place on our Olympic riding team. One day she was training here and her horse took a jump the wrong way. It is inconceivable that it could have been Isabel's fault. She was a superb horsewoman. Later there was an investigation and some people tried to prove that the bars were not set up correctly or that the horse had been scared by something, but nothing was decided for sure. And what did it matter then? I was in a meeting in the city when they called me. Have you ever seen a beautiful bird after it has been mauled by a cat? She had the whole world before her—"

"Don't," Catherine said, putting a hand on his arm. "Don't tell me if it gives you pain."

César shook his head, his dark eyes glistening with emotion. "No, it is better for me if I speak. Even now I must force myself at times to face the tragic fact of how quickly a life can be broken. Sometimes, when I am away from her, I almost pursuade myself that it didn't happen, that when I go back to Los Limonares, Isabel will run out to meet me, as she used to do."

"She is still alive, then."

"Alive, yes," he said bitterly, "but not living, not

really. She sits in her wheelchair all day, holding in her lap a book which she doesn't open. I have tried to convince her to remain in Cali, where she could see more people and have some kind of a life in the community. But she says that no one is interested in her except as an object of curiosity. At first her friends drove out to see her often. But people forget. They forget how long the hours can be for a person who just sits. Isabel says that their desertion of her proves a point, that she would be a charity case in the city, where it would be more convenient for people to come and pity her. It is terrible, her depression. In these three years her mind has become more sick than her body."

"Does she hate visitors?"

César reflected. "No, she is not that far gone yet. She loves to talk to people and when someone does visit, she is happy for the rest of the day. It is simply that she doesn't want her old friends to visit her out of duty; and there is no opportunity to make new ones. Besides, she believes she has lost the ability to be interesting and worthy of friendship in her own right."

"But something must be done. She is too young to become so embittered," Catherine asserted. She hesitated before continuing. "Please don't think I am being forward when I say this, but if there is anything I can do for her, tell me. She must be helped."

For a moment César said nothing, and Catherine feared that she had overstepped the bounds of propriety for a casual acquaintance. Yet she was so moved by her companion's disclosure that she felt compelled to do whatever she could to help him and his sister. At last he said, without looking at her, "Perhaps you could visit her. That is, if I might impose upon your limited amount of time. Isabel is still a very charming person when she is happy, and I think you would not be bored."

Catherine wanted to cry out at the humility of his request. She knew in an instant that, aside from the humanitarian side of the situation, she could never be bored by anything that concerned him. But she said nothing. They stood awhile longer watching the activities around the stables, then in wordless agreement turned to walk back to the clubhouse. She felt a fragile bond between them and feared to destroy it by talk.

César might have felt as she did, for he did not speak again until they were seated with menus on the clubhouse terrace. Below them, at the edge of the golf course, a flock of white ducks dipped and fluttered in a small pond. "You see, it is not so easy to take a holiday from oneself," he said lightly. Catherine concurred with a nod. It was the last reference he made to his sister's tragedy, and for the remainder of lunch he was his old sardonic self.

Catherine said little and tasted less. Everything seemed unreal and dreamlike. She kept stepping outside herself to see Catherine Gray, an ordinary, everyday sort of person, seated in a plush, private club in South America with a man who could be either an international playboy or a hard-bitten tycoon, a man who seemed to have revealed more of himself than he wished yet who remained shrouded in mystery. She understood how Cinderella must have felt as she heard the clock striking midnight, for all too soon she would be back in the workaday world, with not even a glass slipper to remember him by. Once her thoughts were broken when César nodded curtly to a couple through the glass wall of the dining room. Seeing Catherine's eyes follow his glance, he explained, "Since we are on vacation, we will pretend that we know no one, all right? Those people are friends of the family but they would bore you."

After the meal César lit a thin black cigar and they

sat quietly, enjoying the freshening afternoon breeze. He seemed to be absorbed in his own thoughts and once again Catherine was at a loss to know whether he enjoyed her company or was merely tolerating it for reasons of his own. Finally she roused herself to ask, "Isn't it getting late? I really should be getting back, I think. Mrs. Imbert has invited friends for dinner and I promised I would be there when they arrived."

César flicked back his cuff to check the time and summoned the waiter. "There is one more thing I want to show you," he said. "You have plenty of time."

When they were back within the city limits, César directed Leonardo to turn onto a dirt road that rose swiftly up the mountainside. In a short time they had left the scattered houses behind and were crossing the spine of the mountain range. Once around a sharp bend, Catherine could see up ahead the gigantic statue that she had been told was Cristo Rey, Christ the King, which she had seen from afar on the first day as she approached Cali. They came to a stop in the small concrete parking area at the base of the statue. Two other cars were there and some tourists were buying postcards at the small snack bar to one side. Leaving Leonardo with the car, they walked over to the iron railing that bounded the summit and protected the sightseer from the steep decline to the south. The view commanded two very different worlds. Below, the city steamed in the afternoon sun. To the north Catherine saw the gray Andes marching toward the sea. She shivered in the crisp mountain air.

"It's magnificent," she said, "and to think that if you hadn't brought me here, I would have had no idea that the mountains existed. They're completely hidden from below."

He gave a short bow to acknowledge her thanks, then pointed up the valley. "If you know just where to look, and if the day is clear, you can see the beginning of our land. There, to the left of that village, about three quarters of the way up, those are our cane fields—"

"I think I see. You mean where the solid green starts?" Catherine asked. He had put his hand on her shoulder to shift her into a better position and his arm now came to rest across her shoulders, pulling her gently toward him. Without meaning to, Catherine shuddered.

César looked down at her. "You're cold," he said.

The warmth of his body, so close, kindled Catherine's into flame. "I'm not," she replied quickly, turning her head away and looking back toward the car. The tourists were gone and Leonardo was nowhere to be seen. They were alone on top of the world. She started to take a step away but he drew her back to him.

"Little Colt," he taunted, "are you trying to bolt and run? That's what you always do, don't you? I have seen your kind before."

"Let me go," Catherine ordered, irritated by his tone.

"Ah, but you can't escape me," he went on softly. "I know quite a bit about little colts and how to make them behave."

"And how to break them, I suppose!" Catherine snapped.

"Yes, and how to break them."

"You could never break me!" Catherine flashed. Somehow they had turned so that she faced him, standing within the circle of his arms. She put her fists on his chest and pushed. César let her go so quickly that she almost fell backward with the force of her recoil. Then he was standing with his arms folded across his chest, looking very amused. Catherine wondered with sudden embarrassment if she had misinterpreted the

53

whole event. The ground was rocky. Had he been holding on to her merely to steady her footing? He was too sophisticated and too much of a gentleman to force himself on her physically, that she now felt sure of. His verbal trespasses were something else, however.

César Saavedra chuckled, but there was a dangerous light in his eyes. "If I decided to try, that is, *if* I decided to try, I would cure you of that skittishness in no time. But you have nothing to fear."

"I want to go home," Catherine whispered, her eyes downcast.

"Yes, I imagine you do, Little Colt," he drawled. "And far be it from me to stand in the way of your wishes. Shall we depart?" He saw her into the car, then ambled over to the refreshment stand, where the chauffeur was chatting with the proprietress. When the two returned, César gave instructions for the Señorita Gray to be taken home and got in without speaking to his passenger.

Catherine scarcely saw the scenery on the way back, although she was aware that the air became gradually thicker and more humid as they descended, which added to the impression she had had of being in another world atop the mountain. For most of the ride, however, she writhed in an agony of chagrin, certain that she had jumped to conclusions about César's actions at Cristo Rey. In retrospect, the rest of the day seemed almost perfect, yet she, by her stupidity, had brought it to a rather imperfect close. The worst part was that he would think that she had been expecting him to kiss her, that she had been dreaming about him like a silly schoolgirl. She had to admit to herself that subconsciously it might be true. He had a kind of magnetism that at once attracted and threatened her. When she had felt his arm close around her, she must have given into submerged fantasies about his intentions.

When he had said, "But you have nothing to fear," his tone had cut her to the quick. In effect he had told her that she did not hold the slightest attraction for him, and that she was a fool to think she did.

Catherine breathed a sigh of relief when they turned into the Imberts' street, yet almost at once she was assailed by a new distress. She could not think of how she should take leave of César. Before the incident at Cristo Rey she could have thanked him quite naturally for an interesting day. But the memory of her absurd struggle to free herself from him rose between them, a laughing specter, and seemed to render any standard form of politeness inappropriate. She was conscious that she was blushing furiously as she turned to look at him; when she opened her mouth to say she knew not what, he seemed to sense her discomfiture and raised a hand to silence her. Out of his breast pocket he slipped a floridly painted postcard and tendered it to her. He had no doubt bought it when he went into the refreshment stand.

"This card has the same view of the valley that we saw," he said, "and there," tapping with his finger, "is the beginning of the lands held by Los Limonares. You can see it better on the card than you could with the naked eye. Thus does art triumph over nature once again. I thought you might like to have it."

"I do, thank you," Catherine stammered, "and thank you . . . for the day."

"It is I who should thank you," he returned graciously. As soon as she stepped out of the car, he turned away to light another cigar, apparently dismissing her from his concern.

The maid who let Catherine in informed her that the Señora Violet and the Señorita María Lucía were upstairs resting until it was time to get ready for dinner. Catherine went to her room and lay down on the bed, leaving the door ajar so that she would know when her hosts were up and about.

She lay in a kind of daze, wanting to sort out the events of the day and make sense of them, yet unable to begin. From somewhere in her reading, someone's definition of a gentleman came to her. It went, *A gentleman is one who never knowingly causes another person pain.* She tried to apply it to César Saavedra, who would certainly be a gentleman by any other standard. At times during their acquaintance (could it be only three days ago that he had first spoken to her in the airport?) she had thought him cruel. His gibes about Alex had certainly been uncalled for, almost as if he were jealous. That was hardly likely, she reminded herself. Perhaps their clashes were all her fault. Alex, her faithful observer, had said that she sometimes took things too seriously, had even hinted that her sense of humor was not what it should be. Not that Alex's was anything to brag about, she thought with unwonted severity. Maybe César had merely been engaging in harmless banter, flirting with her, and it had been her touchiness that had pushed things onto a more combative plane.

Catherine groaned aloud and rolled over onto her side. Of course that was it. She had always heard that Latins liked to flirt and to compliment a woman. They meant nothing by it except to pass the time pleasantly. He had only been teasing her with his talk of Sleeping Beauty, skittish colts, and the idea that she was afraid of him. He must think her an unutterable bore and a stick-in-the-mud not to have caught on to the spirit of his jesting and to have responded in kind. The only excuse she could offer in her defense was that she was completely out of practice. Alex wasn't the flirting type; and besides, they had known each other too long for that.

"Catherine, are you all right?" María Lucía asked hesitantly from outside the door.

Catherine pushed herself up against the pillow. "Of course I am. Come on in. I just got home and the maid told me you were napping."

María Lucía came in, looking bright-eyed and rested. "I was, but I heard you moan and imagined you had eaten something that didn't agree with you. I forgot to warn you not to eat anything from the street vendors. Tourists invariably get sick, though the people who live here rarely do."

Catherine shook her head. "It isn't that. I was just lying here thinking how dumb I am."

"Why? Did something happen between you and don César? I'm dying to hear about your day. Tell me all about it, especially what he's like. This is probably my only chance to find out!"

"I don't know where to begin," Catherine pondered. "On balance, I guess it was a very nice day. He took me all over the downtown, then out to his club in the country, where we had lunch, then to Cristo Rey, then back here."

"That sounds nice. What did you have for lunch?" asked María Lucía, who could never resist talking about food.

Catherine stopped, surprised. "I don't remember. No, wait a minute, it will come to me—"

María Lucía bounced in her chair with glee. "Oh, Catherine, that's really funny, you know. Now don't try to tell me you aren't interested in him, when you were so absorbed that you didn't even know what you were eating!"

"It was something with chicken in it," Catherine continued doggedly. "No, or maybe it was—oh, now, I'll remember it. I'm just tired."

"Never mind," her friend interjected. "What else happened? Did you talk much?"

"Yes, that's what I was groaning about. I just seem to put my foot in my mouth every time I say something. I think maybe he was trying to be charming, but I didn't give him much of a chance. We seemed to be clashing all the time."

"Sparks flying!"

"Well, not the right kind of sparks," Catherine corrected. "I guess we just don't get along well."

"And yet he keeps coming back for more," María Lucía reminded her. "Are you going to see him again?"

"I don't know. He said something about my visiting Los Limonares once, but that was before"—Catherine halted, unwilling to describe the scene at Cristo Rey—"before we disagreed so much."

"Oh, don't worry. You're too nice to have said anything permanently damaging. But does he know when you're leaving? It would be a shame if he called after you'd gone."

"I never told him the exact date," Catherine remembered. "It didn't seem important for him to know."

"Yoo-hoo!" Violet Imbert tapped at the door, then came into the room. "I'll declare, you're the easiest house guest to entertain! You make your own entertainment! Today you went off with the most eligible male in the valley and tomorrow you're going to see a different side of Colombia entirely, I'm thinking. Have you told Catherine our arrangement, *mija*?"

A look of strain crept into María Lucía's eyes, but she answered lightly, "No, I haven't. Catherine, we thought that it might be more . . . fun tomorrow if the group were a bit larger. Eduardo is coming, too, and bringing a little cousin of ours who likes seeing the cattle and chickens. We sent word to Frank and he said it was all right."

58

"Fine, that sounds good to me," Catherine smiled. Apparently María Lucía's family did not trust her and were sending a chaperon in the person of her brother, Eduardo, rather than call off the excursion. "Tell me again who is coming to dinner tonight," she requested. "I want to get it straight."

"No eligible men; you'll just have to endure our old friends," Violet jested. "There'll be Doctor Delgado and his wife—he and my husband were in school together—and the Gomezes, with their daughter, Patricia, who is a friend of María Lucía's. It has been a tradition for years that we three families dine together during the Christmas season. Which reminds me that I'd better go down to the kitchen and see how the cook is getting along. We haven't much time."

"I'll let you finish your rest," María Lucía said, rising to follow her mother, "and go do something about my hair. See you in a little while."

Catherine lay back with her arms behind her head. She had almost told the Imberts about Isabel, but at the last moment had held back. The facts of the accident they would surely know already from the newspapers. But César's manner of confiding in her, and the kind, sensitive side of his mystifying personality, which he had shown in talking about his sister, Catherine wanted to treasure in silence. She wondered what else she might learn about him. When it was time to get ready for dinner, she stuck the postcard he had given her into a corner of the dressing table mirror and glanced at it from time to time as she dressed, wondering if she would ever see Los Limonares.

CHAPTER FOUR

In spite of her earlier misgivings about the wisdom of the venture, Catherine found herself in good spirits the next morning as she helped to pack the car for the trip to Frank Gibson's farm. Eduardo Imbert, María Lucía's genial, round-faced brother, arrived at the crack of dawn from his bachelor quarters in one of the new high-rise buildings downtown and took charge of the proceedings. Into the car went hampers of sandwiches, hard-boiled eggs, various condiments, and the promised ginger cookies; a case of cold drinks; a stack of *ruanas*; cameras, umbrellas, and empty baskets to fill at the market. Clarita, the Imberts' ten-year-old cousin, danced around the car with excitement and joked with her uncle Eduardo about how many tarantulas she was going to catch. Catherine and María Lucía, dressed in sturdy shoes, jeans, and sweaters against the cooler mountain temperatures, hurried in and out, bringing forgotten purses, cushions, and last-minute additions of pickles and tinned sweets from Violet. At last they piled into the car and roared up the sleeping street, with Eduardo singing a funny Mexican song in a blaring baritone. His good humor was infectious; it was impossible to be nervous or glum around him. Catherine was especially glad he had come, for his bantering seemed to relax María Lucía.

The road out of the city was fairly free of traffic at that hour, so Eduardo fit the pace of the car to Catherine's interest in the scenery. Just as they were leaving the city limits she cried out suddenly, causing him to slam on the brakes so fast that Clarita, in the backseat, tumbled to the floor.

"I'm sorry," Catherine said, "but the bus!" She pointed after a lumbering local bus, whose roof was heaped with bundle upon bundle of large purple flowers.

"But you've seen a bus before," Eduardo said.

"But—it's like something out of a dream," Catherine insisted.

Eduardo said, "Oh, you mean the flowers. Yes, they cut them in the mountains early this morning and are bringing them down to sell. It's good to have you with us, Catherine. You make us look at things we no longer see, because we have grown so accustomed to them." He chuckled as he put the car in gear again, so Catherine knew he wasn't angry with her.

The road became so steep and winding that Eduardo soon had to abandon conversation and concentrate on driving. Catherine herself felt silenced by the growing majesty of the terrain. For a time the highway traveled on the walls of a deep, narrow valley. Far below, Catherine could see tiny houses and paths, seemingly unconnected to any village or thoroughfare, and she wondered what kind of life went on in such isolation. She was also led to ask herself why Frank Gibson had elected to bury himself in such a remote area. Perhaps he had been won by just such savage beauty as she was seeing. She could understand that, for she had always

61

preferred any countryside to the city. Farther on they came to a pleasantly wooded plateau, dotted with charming houses that, María Lucía explained, were summer homes of Cali residents.

"Many people who live and work in the city have small weekend farms up here. Frank bought one of them and is hoping to make it pay," she said.

"A stubborn man," Eduardo said shortly, causing Catherine to wonder whether he was referring to Frank's farming or to something else. However, she thought it best not to ask any questions and instead turned to Clarita and passed the time talking about the child's schoolwork.

In the mountains the day was misty and gray. Feeling the breeze from the open window, Catherine realized that her face was lightly beaded with moisture.

"This is the highest point," Eduardo announced as they passed several restaurants and a police station. "It is known simply as Kilometer Eighteen. We have climbed about three thousand feet in the last half hour and will now start down the other side of this range. It's not far now."

The vegetation had grown lush, with a hint of the jungle about it. Catherine began to look more closely at the modest houses, most with red tile roofs and wooden walls, trying to guess which would be Frank's. Then Clarita cried, "There he is!" and Catherine saw Frank in front of a white frame house that perched on a lip of land overlooking the blue-green valley. Frank looked up and waved as they turned off the main road. He had been checking the engine of a battered pickup truck and now slammed down the hood and came toward them.

"Wonderful morning, isn't it?" he said briskly, shaking hands first with Eduardo, then with Catherine and María Lucía, and tousling Clarita's hair. "I think we'd better go to the market in my old bus so we'll have room for what we buy. I was planning to get my food for the week."

"Of course," Eduardo agreed. "Can we put some things in the house first?" To Catherine's watchful eye, he appeared cordial enough.

Everyone lent a hand in transferring the picnic supplies inside. Catherine moved slowly, observing everything. A fence of thick bamboo poles enclosed the front yard, which was a crazy quilt of impatiens, salvia, day lilies, and rosebushes. Outside the fence grew carnations, red and white, and the heavy purple flowers she had seen atop the bus.

"This is like a Munchkin garden!" she exclaimed as she passed Frank on the stone walk. "You know, in *The Wizard of Oz*. I almost expect to see the magic shoes of the Wicked Witch of the West sticking out from under the house. Did you plant all this?"

Frank laughed and scratched his head. "No, it was all here when I came. I try to take care of the flowers, but I'm afraid I don't even know their names, much less how to care for them. Elena, the wife of my hired man, says the place needs a woman's touch. Uh, just take that box into the kitchen."

The inside of the house was almost primitive in its simplicity, yet Catherine could imagine that it suited its owner very well. To the left of the living room ran a long hall, which led to the bedrooms. To the right lay the kitchen and another room, which Frank obviously used as a tack room, for through its doorway she spied saddles, cinches, and articles pertaining to livestock neatly ranged along the walls. The walls of the living room were hung with handsome cowhides and native blankets in the rich, muted colors of vegetable dyes. Coarse wool rugs woven with Indian designs covered parts of the painted wood floor. The furniture was sparse: a big table painted blue and white and a few chairs, augmented by a long, built-in bench that ran under the picture window. Catherine went to it and knelt on the chintz cushions that lined it. She leaned her elbows on the sill and looked down. Far, far below, the tumbling hillside came to a temporary halt before plunging to the valley floor. There, on a roughly circular field, she saw several specks moving and finally made them out to be horses. Standing there, so isolated, they seemed to be outside time.

"I'll take you down there later," a voice said, and Catherine glanced over her shoulder to discover Frank watching her. "Like what you see?"

"Yes," Catherine answered, "but you're crazy to try to farm it."

Frank chuckled. "Now that's what I like, a girl who's a realist."

"I'm not a realist, I'm a farmer's daughter," Catherine pointed out. "That's a nice job of terracing, though." She referred to a series of vegetable beds that had been sculpted in stair-step fashion out of the slope immediately below the window.

Frank nodded enthusiastically and came to sit beside her. "Yes, I'm really proud of that. The strawberries are taking hold there now. Just give me another year and—"

At that moment María Lucía appeared at the door and announced, a bit sharply, "We're ready to leave." Catherine's first thought was that her friend had been watching them through the window and did not want them to be alone together. Quickly she dismissed the idea. If the day was to be a success, she must put all thoughts of romantic complications to one side. And if Frank and María Lucía were playing a game with each other, she refused to be a pawn in it. However, she found it hard to believe that there were any hidden motives in Frank's behavior. He seemed as carefree as the sunlit landscape outside. María Lucía was something else. Catherine had once known her as well as she knew herself. But she reminded herself that people change and that love can do strange things to one.

When she stepped outside, Eduardo directed, "You two girls ride up front with Frank. I've put cushions in the back for Clarita and me. We'll hold on to Trapper." He gestured at a full-grown German shepherd who sat quietly in the bed of the truck. Catherine, who had not noticed the dog when they arrived, went over to admire the sleek animal. Trapper lowered his head at her touch and nuzzled her arm.

Frank paused beside her and said approvingly, "You're used to animals, aren't you? I can tell by the way you handle Trapper."

"Oh, yes, we've always had setters on the farm, and sometimes beagles. I used to go hunting with my father just to handle the dogs."

"You go hunting? Miss Gray, you're full of surprises," Frank said. He swung in the cab and coaxed the motor to life. Catherine hung back, stroking the dog, until María Lucía was seated in the middle, then took the window seat. María Lucía did not look pleased at the favor Catherine had found in Frank's eyes.

Frank turned west onto the highway. "I guess somebody's told you those are banana trees," he said for Catherine's benefit, pointing to a stand of trees with enormous leaves. "And up there on that hill—you see those plants with spiky leaves?—those are hemp plants. They pound the leaves to get the hemp fibers out and then dry those in the sun and make rope from them. You'll see the drying racks as we go along." He stopped talking while he veered across the center line to pass two boys riding bareback on an old horse, then asked, "What's the matter, María? Cat got your tongue?"

A spark of María Lucía's customary vivacity returned as she said coyly, "Oh, no, Frank, I just don't want to interrupt your travelogue. You know more about Colombia than I do."

"You just seem kind of quiet today," Frank noted. "Tell me what you two girls have been up to. Have you done much sightseeing?"

"Catherine spent all day yesterday sightseeing, but not with us," María Lucía said archly.

"Oh, how's that? Did some of your mother's friends take her?"

"We-ell," María Lucía began hesitantly, as if she were trying to put her explanation as delicately as possible, "you see, Catherine made a friend at the airport, before she even arrived at our house, and that gentleman took her out yesterday. Wasn't that lucky for her?"

"The people here are unusually hospitable," Catherine said stiffly. She could see the day turning into an ordeal if María Lucía was going to make snide remarks about her in order to protect her own interests with Frank. Somehow she must get María Lucía off to one side and remind her how unnecessary her fears were. Surely she must realize that Catherine's commitment to Alex rendered other possibilities quite impossible. But María Lucía was speaking again, determined to make the most of her opportunity.

"This gentleman friend happens to be quite an important person in the valley. Have you heard of César Saavedra?"

Frank furrowed his brow. "Isn't there a coffee exporting company called Saavedra?"

"It's the same family," María Lucía affirmed. "César's brother runs it in Bogotá. César runs the big sugar cane plantation on the road to Palmira."

Frank shook his head in disgust. "Those big land-owners! What this country needs is a more equitable distribution of wealth. Those fellows take everything and don't give anything back."

"That's not true! He isn't like that!" The words were out of Catherine's mouth before she knew she was going to say them. Frank and María Lucía both looked at her quizzically.

"Why, how could you possibly know? You've only just met him," María Lucía said sweetly, looking pleased with herself.

"I just know," Catherine answered, setting her chin.

"Look, it's a complex subject," Frank said generously. "I probably shouldn't have brought it up. Eduardo knows more about it than any of us. Why don't we wait and ask him?"

Catherine saw that Frank had stopped discussion in order not to embarrass her and threw him a grateful glance. Perhaps he was not so unaware of the tension in the air as she had thought. But why had she burst out in César's defense? She knew nothing about him as a businessman and little more about him as a human being. More importantly, why did she care what people thought of him? Still, she felt that her reaction had been correct. Somehow she did know that he was an honorable man, a man who would be aware of the responsibilities of his position and wouldn't shirk them. She could almost hear César laughing at her for her outburst. He would be the first to tell her that he needed no help in defending himself. She wondered what Frank knew about him; the family seemed to be legendary in the valley.

They were passing more and more mountain people along the roadside. Most were walking with the steady, swinging stride of people who were used to doing all their traveling by foot; but there was a scattering of people on horses and mules as well. They were all headed for the market and many were dressed in their best clothes. Frank braked and motioned to a group to climb in the back of the truck. Two men started forward, but at the sight of Trapper they shook their heads and backed away.

"If they only knew!" Frank laughed. "Trapper really is man's best friend. Most dogs that size have been trained as watchdogs, and I guess they think he's pretty ferocious. But Trapper is just too nice to bite anyone." Clarita rapped on the window of the cab and laughingly called their attention to the big dog, who had curled up with his muzzle resting morosely on his paws, oblivious to the reaction he had provoked.

When they came to a cluster of buildings, too small even to be called a village, Frank pulled the truck off the road. Ahead Catherine saw a wide field where a crowd milled around in a maze of makeshift stalls and tables heaped with merchandise. Clarita bolted out of the truck like a young rabbit and bounded ahead, turning to urge Eduardo to follow her. Frank got out and fastened a strong leash to Trapper's collar.

"I'm going on with Eduardo and Clarita," María Lucía announced, taking a basket on her arm. She looked back as she walked slowly away, but if she had been expecting Frank to call after her, her hopes were disappointed. He bustled around the truck, checking the glove compartment, locking doors, and setting out market baskets, whistling all the while.

"Here, you hold Trapper a minute," he ordered, handing the leash to Catherine. She took it reluctantly, for she was afraid that staying with Frank meant angering María Lucía. But what else could she do? The others had been swallowed up by the crowd and there was no catching up with them. For an instant she considered speaking to Frank about María Lucía, but

quickly abandoned the idea. Even if she had understood what was going on, which she didn't, the affair
was none of her business. She watched Frank as he
moved around the truck, checking the tires. Whatever
María Lucía was trying to tell him, he wasn't getting
the message.

Frank came toward her, dusting his hands on his
jeans. "Everything looks fine. When I start making a
real profit, I'll have to put some of it into truck repairs,
though. Let's go."

The market was a chaotic mixture of farm produce
and notions, unlike anything Catherine had seen.
Stacks of bright, cheap clothing, live chickens, tables of
rusty tools, piles of vegetables, and trays of combs and
jewelry all vied for the buyer's attention. She concluded
that the people from the surrounding hills must depend
upon it for nearly all of their needs. Frank seemed to
be a great favorite with some of the stallkeepers.

"Ah, señor," one of the women greeted him. "Every
week I ask you where is your sweetheart and finally
you have brought her!"

"No, no," Frank laughed. "You're always trying to
marry me off."

"That's not your sweetheart?" the woman demanded, looking Catherine up and down. "Why not?"

"Aren't you interested in selling anything today?"
Frank countered. "How much are your carrots?"

The woman laughed and threw up her hands, "For
you I have a special price. How many do you want?"

Many of the fruits and vegetables were unknown to
Catherine and she listened eagerly as Frank, a born
teacher, patiently took up the items one by one and explained their uses and growing habits. At one of the
fruit stands he took out a heavy clasp knife and split
and peeled a mango for them to share. The sweet,
slightly stringy pulp tasted to Catherine like flowers.

Adept at bargaining, though not ruthless, Frank had the market baskets groaning with produce before long.

As he happily dickered over the price of potatoes Catherine stood to one side and observed the way he towered over the smaller, darker Colombians. She tried to imagine what it would be like if Alex were with her. He wouldn't approve of the meat hanging in the open air or of the mud underfoot, of that she was certain. Strangely, she had never before considered what it would be like to travel with Alex. Surely they would take vacations after they were married, although she had to admit that it was already difficult to get him away from the store. She wondered if her fiancé would enjoy himself as much as she was just then. Alex didn't like surprises and he was always making lists and schedules so as not to waste a minute of his time. No, the kind of aimless strolling and people-watching she and Frank were doing would not appeal to Alex, whose activities had to point toward specific goals. She herself liked to let a place or an experience take hold of her slowly.

Unbidden, the image of César Saavedra rose up before her again and she remembered the way they had walked together in the city, stopping and going on in a kind of unconscious accord, neither hindered by the other's pace. There had been some very comfortable moments with him, when Catherine had felt completely at ease with herself and with César. But so far they had seen each other in rather artificial situations, and she found herself longing to see him at home and to know what an ordinary day of his life was like. She wondered what he was doing that morning and if he was alone. Would he fit into the rough-and-tumble of the marketplace, where Frank was so at home? It was strange that César Saavedra had never married.

A sharp pull on Trapper's leash brought Catherine

back to her surroundings. She had taken the dog again while Frank was bargaining but had allowed the leash to go slack as she pursued her thoughts. Thus she had not seen the huge brindled mongrel that had halted a few feet away. Trapper lunged against his collar in an effort to get at the cur and at the same time broke into frenzied barking. People drew back, anticipating a fight, and Catherine suddenly found herself alone in a muddy circle. The brindled cur sidled toward them, growling low in the throat and curling its lip up over long, yellowed fangs. No one claimed it or called it back. Catherine threw her weight against the leash and tried to pull Trapper backward, but the big animal strained forward with enormous strength.

"Trapper! Heel!" she said sharply, but the dog paid no attention. Slowly, inexorably, she felt her feet give way in the soft ground as Trapper inched toward the mongrel. The other dog crouched with its belly to the ground, bunching itself for a leap. Trapper stopped, shivering slightly. The hair on his neck bristled. In the instant that both dogs fell silent, Catherine realized in terror that they were seconds away from tangling. Already she felt in anticipation the shock of their heavy bodies colliding. A boy shouted in excitement. She stood paralyzed, unable to exert more force.

"Back!" A hand closed over her own and Trapper was jerked backward head over paws. Without releasing his hold, Frank Gibson surged forward menacingly, so that the other dog slunk reluctantly away, uttering an occasional flurry of barks to salvage his self-respect. Frank laughed and nodded to the appreciative bystanders, who quickly turned back to their bargaining.

"Are you all right? I shouldn't have left you to handle him," Frank said, patting Catherine's shoulder the way one comforts a child. The great dog stood close against his leg, once again the obedient companion. "Sorry to be so rough with you, boy," his master apologized.

Catherine ran a hand through her hair. She felt shaky in the knees but said, "I'm fine, but it's a good thing you stepped in when you did. It could have been nasty." She saw María Lucía, Eduardo, and Clarita coming toward them, doubtless attracted by the commotion.

"I'm really sorry about it," Frank was saying earnestly. "I could never have forgiven myself if something had happened to you."

"Oh, I meant it would have been nasty for Trapper," Catherine rejoined hastily. "I would have stepped aside." In so saying, she stepped out from under Frank's comforting hand. She hoped María Lucía had not seen and heard Frank's expressions of concern, for she was sure to give them a wrong interpretation. Unfortunately it appeared that the girl had heard, for her face was suffused with an angry flush. Nevertheless she managed to ask, "Are you hurt? Someone said—"

"Oh, for heaven's sake, let's forget it," Catherine said. "Where have you been? I wanted to see everything with you."

María Lucía eyed her doubtfully, obviously believing that Catherine would rather be left alone with Frank, but just then Frank suggested, "Let's all stick together for a while," and Catherine silently blessed his diplomacy. She noticed how closely Eduardo was following his sister and reflected that Trapper was not the only watchdog present. They continued meandering through the market. Once Eduardo stopped to buy a straw hat for Clarita and farther on Frank ordered some bones to be wrapped up for Trapper. After a while Catherine found herself standing before a tarpaulin that had been spread out on the ground to display a variety of curious objects.

72

"What is all this?" she whispered to María Lucía as she looked askance at the somber young man who seemed to be in charge.

"These are charms and supposedly magical cures," her friend returned. "That thing in the bowl to the left is a hairball from a cow's stomach, guaranteed to ward off witches. The pamphlets tell how to recognize the devil if you should happen to meet him, and those herbs promise to cure everything from the common cold to flat feet. He does a good business among the peasants."

"The señorita wishes to have her fortune told?" The young man addressed Catherine in Spanish. His modern haircut and clothes mixed oddly with his bronzed face, which had the flat planes and impassiveness of a pre-Columbian statue.

"Me?" Catherine asked in surprise. "Oh, no, no, I was just looking at your wares. Very interesting."

"The señorita must have her fortune told," he stated and turned to call someone behind him.

"What does he mean?" Catherine asked hurriedly. "I don't want to have my fortune told. Why is he so serious?"

"Come on, then, let's go," giggled María Lucía. "That's all part of his selling pitch. He pretends to know something you don't."

A tiny, gray-haired woman had materialized beside the young man. With a self-effacing smile, which was brightened by two gold front teeth, she held out her hand. "If the señorita would show me her palm . . . ?"

"No, thank you, not today," María Lucía said firmly.

But Catherine suddenly interjected, "Wait a minute. Why not?" She held forth her palm and the old woman took it between her own clawlike hands and studied it closely. The fine web of wrinkles about her eyes deepened and drew together as she concentrated. At length she looked up, measuring Catherine shrewdly. "You have traveled over water——"

"That's not hard to figure out," remarked Frank, who had stopped to watch.

"——and you want to find a certain thing," the old woman went on imperturbably. "You are one of those who search. You are looking for it very hard."

"And will I find it?" Catherine asked half-seriously.

The woman referred again to the outstretched palm. After an ominous pause she said, "You do not yet know what you are looking for. But it will come, it will come. You will not see your homeland again for a long time."

"Oh, my," Catherine said mildly to María Lucía, "think of all the money I could have saved by buying a one-way ticket."

They paid the fortune-teller and strolled away, chuckling at the woman's gravity. "At least she believes it herself," Eduardo remarked. "And she probably has a certain amount of influence in her village. Some of these people depend on palm readings and other signs to govern their lives."

It was after midday when they returned to Frank's house. Frank and Eduardo immediately set about building a fire in the outdoor fireplace, while Catherine and María Lucía unpacked the picnic.

"Hurry, hurry, I'm starving," Clarita begged, hopping from one foot to the other.

"Here, take a sandwich," María Lucía suggested. "Frank is going to cook steaks, so it will be a while. Why don't you ask him if you can feed the chickens?"

The child scampered off, leaving Catherine and María Lucía together on the long porch, where the table from inside had been placed for the meal. María Lucía worked silently, her features inscrutable. Catherine, noting that Frank and Eduardo were out of earshot for

74

the moment, said quickly, "I enjoyed seeing the market so much, except that . . . I'm worried about you. Are you all right? Do you regret coming very much?"

María Lucía looked up, startled. Seeing that she had caught her friend off guard, Catherine pursued her advantage. "I didn't come all the way to South America to spend time with Frank Gibson or anyone else but you; surely you know that. I wish you wouldn't run off and leave me with him so much."

"I didn't want to be—what is the expression—a fifth wheel," María Lucía said. "You two seem to get along well together. You did from the very beginning."

"It's easy to get along with Frank. Anybody could," Catherine argued. "Look, if you still care about him, why not give yourself a chance? Instead of disappearing, stay around and talk to him. Just be natural."

"Eduardo—" María Lucía began.

"Mmmm, I'd forgotten about him," Catherine admitted. Then, also forgetting that she had forsworn romantic intrigue, she winked at María Lucía. "Why don't I take Eduardo off your hands for a while? I have so many questions about the flora and fauna of Colombia that I'll bet it would take your brother all afternoon to answer them."

"Would you?" María Lucía pleaded, her voice dropping to a whisper as Clarita raced up again to snag a piece of fruit. "It would mean so much to me. With a little time, perhaps I could get an idea of how Frank feels—"

"Just leave it to me," Catherine whispered back.

By the time they had finished arranging the table, Catherine was certain that she had repaired much of the damage to María Lucía's feelings. Her next task would be to show Frank in a kind way that she was not available and to keep Eduardo from watching over his sister so closely and making her self-conscious. The role was new to her, for she was neither devious nor scheming by nature, but her sense of justice and fair play rebelled against the strictures placed on María Lucía. Besides, she could not bear to see her friend of so many years unhappy. She was determined to do what she could to improve the situation, so long as she did not involve herself in a quarrel with the Imberts. Her intuition told her that Frank was not so indifferent to María Lucía as he appeared.

The bracing mountain air, laced with the aroma of broiling steak, whetted appetites keenly, and, in turn, hearty eating relaxed the party and put everyone in a convivial mood. Frank presided over the meal with quaint bachelor awkwardness, apologizing for the mismatched plates he offered and the chairs of different heights. At the end of the meal he proudly brought out a milky white cheese wrapped in banana leaves, which had been made on the farm. Catherine appreciated his pleasure in his own product, for she had often seen the same look on her father's face when he carried in a particularly fine basket of apples or potatoes to show her mother.

"After such a feast, I feel like taking a walk," she said at last. "Anyone want to come? Eduardo? Clarita?"

"Yes, a walk would be good just now," Eduardo agreed. "We can go down to the lower pasture, can't we, Frank?"

"Sure, go right ahead," Frank urged, making no move to join them. Apparently he had forgotten, or had decided against, his earlier invitation to take Catherine on a tour of his land.

"I'll clean up the table," María Lucía offered, and Catherine was glad to see that Eduardo did not insist she come.

Steps had been cut in the hillside next to the house.

Catherine, Eduardo, and Clarita stepped gingerly down the mossy stairs, which the shade of the house had made damp and slippery. Then they climbed down a long slope covered with coarse, wiry grass and low bushes. Narrow trails scored with hoofprints criss-crossed their path.

"Look, there are the cattle," Clarita said, and Catherine spotted a group of them under some trees to the east. Compared to those at home, they were lean and tough-looking.

"Do you see the humps on their backs?" Eduardo asked. "Those cattle are called *criollos*. They are a mixture of Brahmans, or *cebús,* as we call them, and holsteins."

"What a strange combination!" exclaimed Catherine.

"Yes, they are a Colombian compromise," Eduardo nodded. "With that mixture they can withstand heat well, like the Brahmans, yet still produce some meat and milk."

"But these look so thin," Catherine commented.

Eduardo shook his head. "I am a city boy, and I admit I don't know much about ranching, but I think Frank Gibson has his work cut out for him." He looked back toward the house. The back of it rested on stilts and the whole structure looked ready to topple into the valley.

"He seems to be a hard worker," Catherine remarked.

"Yes, but this would be no life for—well, can you imagine someone like María Lucía living in a house that doesn't even have hot water?" he demanded.

Eduardo appeared to be offering his sister's name as a random example, but Catherine knew that he was really telling her how unsuitable a partner Frank would make for his sister. From there, she reasoned that Frank must have been a real threat for Eduardo to continue being concerned after a whole year. Adopting what she hoped was an innocent tone, she said, "Perhaps you underestimate your sister. I remember once when she stayed with my family at hog-killing time. She watched every step of the operation and even helped to render the lard. And did she tell you about driving the neighbor's tractor?"

"My little sister?" Eduardo asked incredulously. Then he reassured himself, "Well, no doubt it was fun during a vacation. But to work hard every day and deny oneself pleasures, that is something else. I'm not sure that my sister has ever even made her own bed, at least at home. There has always been a maid to do it."

"Is that so? She always did at our house," Catherine informed him. As she kept an eye on Clarita, who was offering a handful of grass to one of the cows, she pondered a set of values that required women to be so protected from everyday tasks. She herself would find it hard to get used to such a life, and in fact was not sure that she would enjoy it. She liked domestic chores and had always looked forward to the day when she could have a home of her own to keep neat and shining. However, one could feel protected and cared for even while scrubbing floors. Then, too, Eduardo was forgetting that even a sheltered girl might willingly undergo discomforts to be with someone she loved. It was better not to mention that, Catherine decided.

They had continued walking as they talked and before long reached the circular plateau that Catherine had noticed from above earlier in the day. The horses were gone, but the sense of timelessness remained. The air was still and the sun's rays poured down like liquid brass. Below them lay jungle, where the silvery plumes of the eucalyptus trees stood out against dark green. The three companions sat on a flat rock ledge and basked in the heat, which was welcome after the dampness near the house.

They sat so long that Catherine was nearly lulled to sleep by the peace. Then Eduardo glanced at his watch. "Almost four o'clock," he announced. "Look, the fog is coming down. It does every day about this time. We'd better start back." An even, white curtain was descending the mountain and it looked as if it would soon engulf the house. The mountainside was so steep that they had scrambled a long way down in a short time. As they climbed back up, the distance seemed twice as far; even the lively Clarita was winded by the time they gained the yard. A heavy mist swam about them and Catherine wrapped her jacket closer. Looking back, she saw nothing of their place in the sun, only a white ocean.

Frank came out on the porch to greet them. "I was about to send Trapper out for you. It wouldn't do to fall over a ledge in this fog. Come in and have some hot chocolate. María Lucía has it all ready."

They carried the thick mugs of chocolate out to the porch. Disembodied noises floated to them through the drifting whiteness: an automobile horn, grinding gears, a shout, the faraway barking of a dog.

"Those roses," Catherine said lazily, "the lavender ones. Do they have a name? It's an unusual color for roses."

Frank stepped out into the yard, where the moist air had brought the colors of the flowers up to a blaze. With his clasp knife he sliced off a long stem bearing one silvery purple rose and brought it back to her.

"I don't know what these are called, but why don't we give them a name? I hereby pronounce this the Catherine Rose, in honor of your visit."

"Oh, no," Catherine murmured, taking the flower with reluctance. "No, you shouldn't do that."

"Why not?" Frank returned cheerfully. "The Catherine Rose it is, from now on."

Not daring to look at María Lucía, Catherine managed to thank Frank, but she marveled at how anyone could be so thoughtless. She was glad when, a few minutes later, Eduardo decided that the fog had thinned enough to permit driving. No one in the car, not even Clarita, who fell asleep, said anything until they rolled into the Imberts' garage. As Catherine got out of the car Eduardo called her back. "Don't forget the Catherine Rose," he said, taking up the flower, which she had tossed on top of the dashboard. "You might want to press the petals and save them." As he handed it to her with a flourish, his face was the picture of smirking self-satisfaction. María Lucía stalked past them into the house.

CHAPTER FIVE

The seed had been planted by the old woman at the market. That night, as Catherine and María Lucía sat talking in their nightgowns, Catherine mused, "Why do you suppose the boy at the market insisted that I have my fortune told? Why not you? And why did the old lady say what she did to me? I don't believe any of it, you understand, but I wonder how they decide what to say to each person."

"As for why they singled you out instead of me," María Lucía responded, "it may only have been that you looked more like a tourist and thus more susceptible. But Eduardo has a theory about fortune-telling." She appeared to be quietly pleased with the time spent with Frank, in spite of the incident of the Catherine Rose, and was once more friendly toward her guest. "One day, when our friend Amelia was studying law, she went to a fortune-teller just for fun. Amelia looked very serious as usual, wearing glasses and carrying a bag of books. The fortune-teller told her that she would have five children and live on a ranch in the *llanos,* the plains."

"And did she?" Catherine asked.

"No," María Lucía said, "Amelia finished her studies and became a lawyer. But I don't think she's very happy. Maybe the prophecy will still come true, or should have. Eduardo says that the fortune-teller sizes up the customer, then makes up a prophecy that is very unlikely to happen to a person of that appearance. He claims that our dreams concern what we are not, and that when we go to a fortune-teller, what we want to hear is some assurance that our wildest dreams can come true."

"So in my case," Catherine reasoned, "I must have looked like a person who is content to stay at home and let events take their own course. Goodness, do I look that dull? Anyway, the fortune-teller therefore told me that I was searching for something and that I would not return home for a long time."

"I suppose it would work that way, yes," María Lucía agreed. "But furthermore, according to Eduardo's theory, in your innermost self you really want to travel and to seek adventure, instead of leading a quiet life." She giggled mischievously. "I think the old woman was right. Remember all the silly things we used to daydream about when we were in school? I was the one who wanted to live in a little vine-covered cottage in the country—I was so sentimental about taking care of baby chicks and lambs!—and you wanted to marry a ship's captain and live in the China Sea."

Catherine grinned sheepishly at the memory of their adolescent fantasies. Then she yawned and got to her feet. "Well, Eduardo's theory is interesting, anyway. If you'll excuse me, I think I'll go to bed. I can't think why I'm so sleepy."

"It's probably the shift in climate and altitude we experienced today. I feel the same way. Good night, and don't forget that tomorrow you see your first bullfight."

＊　　＊　　＊

The next morning, as Catherine breakfasted in her room, she found herself idly pondering the course of her life over the past few years. Every Friday evening, as unfailing as the sunset, Alex appeared after dinner to take her shopping or to a movie. Every Sunday noon found the two of them having dinner with Alex's parents and his unmarried brother, Ralph. On Wednesday afternoons Alex didn't work at the store, so he picked her up after school and took her home, usually coming in for a cup of coffee with Catherine and her mother. Within the past year, however, he had been staying on at the store as often as not on Wednesdays. Tuesday evenings Catherine attended the Book Lovers' Circle. She had been the youngest member until last year, when a young mother, who had been two years behind her in school, had joined. Some of the members had been in the Circle thirty years or more. The rest of the week was taken up with her teaching duties and with helping out her parents with the farm chores.

Without interrupting her train of thought, Catherine wrapped her light travel robe more securely about her, gathered up her toilet articles, and started down the hall to take a shower. Passing the head of the stairs, she stopped to greet Violet, who was returning from downstairs and appeared to have been up for hours.

"Good morning, dear," she greeted Catherine. "The mountain air yesterday put roses in your cheeks."

"I did sleep very well," Catherine declared. She started to walk on, but turned back to ask hesitantly, "Before you met your husband . . . what were you planning to do with your life? I mean, marrying and moving to another country must have changed your plans considerably."

"Goodness me, yes," exclaimed Violet. "I had a good job with a publishing company and was writing

83

poetry on the side. Both enterprises were quite successful, I don't mind telling you. I had just been promoted in the publishing firm and several magazines had begun to show an interest in my poems. There was even talk of collecting them into a book. An old beau of mine knew an agent who knew an editor who—well, anyway, I was beginning to make contacts. But then I met Carlos through some friends when he came to New York on business, and all of a sudden nothing seemed to matter except Carlos. So when he finally asked me to marry him and come here, I came without a backward glance."

Picturing the shy, balding don Carlos, Catherine repressed a smile and thought how love, like beauty, is in the eye of the beholder. "But wasn't it a hard decision," she insisted, "changing the direction of your life so completely?"

"I really can't say that there was any decision involved at all. I simply felt an overwhelming conviction that marrying Carlos was the right thing to do, and I acted on it. If that makes me an incurable romantic, then so be it," Violet said, thumping the stair rail for emphasis.

"I think it sounds wonderful," Catherine offered.

"I can't explain what it's like, that feeling of certainty about the future. But if it ever happens to you, you'll recognize it at once," Violet said. "You hear about people agonizing over such decisions, but in my experience, if you have to force yourself to choose, then maybe neither alternative is right."

"But one can't just think of oneself. There may be other people to consider," Catherine said.

"And sometimes," Violet said with conviction, "people pretend to consider other people's feelings when in fact they are afraid to face their own. No, first you must help yourself before you can help others."

"I suppose you're right," Catherine said. She had the feeling that Violet was trying to tell her something quite apart from the spoken content of the conversation.

Just then, Violet brought the meeting to a close. "Right now, the only future that concerns me is a long morning of doing the household accounts. We'll set out for the bullring about two thirty." As Catherine continued down the hall, Violet called after her, "And I kept up my poetry, anyway. If something is important enough to you, you find a way to keep it."

When she had showered and dressed, Catherine sat down to write postcards. She would be home before some of them reached their destinations, but she wanted her friends to know they had been remembered during her trip. She made a point of writing to Alex's parents, who would be quick to call her down if she did not, as well as to Alex. She had completed three cards when she was called to the telephone.

"Catherine? I'm glad to find that you are still here. It occurred to me that I don't know for how long you are staying."

"Good morning, César," Catherine said, her pulse leaping. "Yes, the time has gone so fast. I only have three days left."

"Only three days? I hope you can spare one of them for me. My sister, Isabel, is looking forward to meeting you, so we would like you to come to Los Limonares tomorrow."

"Are you calling from there now?"

"No, no, I had to come to the city this morning; otherwise I would have asked you to come today."

"It's just as well you didn't. The Imberts are taking me to the bullfights this afternoon."

"Good, it's something you should see. There are some excellent matadors here this year. But what do you think? Can you make it tomorrow?"

"Tomorrow night is New Year's Eve—María Lucía and I are going to a party—"

"We will have you back in time for that."

"Well, all right, then. Yes. And thank you for inviting me."

"Until tomorrow, then, at ten?"

"Until tomorrow, César."

Catherine hung up the telephone and bounded up the stairs to find María Lucía. Just saying his name aloud had caused her heart to skip a beat. She hoped she hadn't sounded too eager on the phone. She felt like a sixteen-year-old, like a lark in spring, like anything but herself. It was silly to be so excited over a telephone call, but she didn't care. He wanted to see her again. For the last time, a voice reminded her, for the last time. In three days she would be on her way home. But she shut the little voice out and grinned at the way he had not told her his name, assuming rightly that she would know his voice. Even his arrogance had its endearing side. And he had sounded so busy, so short of time. What was he doing today? Who cared? Tomorrow he would be with her. She beat a sharp rat-a-tat-tat on María Lucía's door and heard her friend answer. María Lucía finished tightening a pearl earring and turned from the mirror. Before she could speak, Catherine asked, as casually as she could manage, "Is it all right if I go out to César's plantation tomorrow morning? He just called and I'm afraid I said yes without thinking. Do we have other plans? I'll be back before the New Year's Eve party."

"There's nothing that can't wait. Of course you must go," María Lucía said firmly. "My, you must be happy."

But Catherine frowned. "I don't know what's the matter with me. I should have asked first before accepting the invitation. You must think me terribly discourteous."

"Don't think of yourself as a guest, but as one of the family," María Lucía said as she turned round and round to observe the swirl of her dress in the mirror. "Besides, I probably would have done the same."

"You are just too gracious to tell me if I am interfering with your plans," Catherine teased.

From the way María Lucía blushed, Catherine knew she had hit the truth. But her friend merely said, "Don't worry about it. I have to put in a couple of hours at the office this morning, but I'll be back at lunchtime. *Hasta luego.*"

After María Lucía had left, Catherine remained sitting in her friend's bedroom for a few moments. The initial exhilaration at hearing from César had subsided, leaving her subdued. She felt uneasy, unlike herself, as if she were losing control over her thoughts and actions. Where there had been only smooth, certain routine in her life before, now there stretched ahead a curving road with question marks at every turn. Why, for instance, had she leaped at César's invitation with no consideration for the Imberts, who had made daily plans for her visit? It was not even the first time she had done so. Why did the thought of going home fill her with confusion? Teaching was her great love, yet she had given her class scarcely a thought, had not even taken photographs or bought souvenirs to share with them. Of late she had become completely self-absorbed, examining her emotions, her daydreams, and her appearance with equal attention. And always, always as she did so, her efforts turned around a single query: What would César Saavedra think about this or that? It was pointless. It was worse than pointless; it was foolish, it was immature, and it was disloyal to Alex.

Catherine went into the hall and knocked on Violet's door. As she entered she said in a rush, "Mrs. Imbert,

87

I think I owe you and María Lucía an apology. I just accepted an invitation to visit César at Los Limonares tomorrow, and now I'm afraid I've upset your plans—"

Violet Imbert whipped off a pair of tortoiseshell reading glasses, leaned her elbows on her desk, and squinted sharply at her guest. "Sit down, dear," she said, motioning to an armchair covered in rose velvet. She pushed a stack of papers to one side as Catherine was seating herself, then went on. "Now, then, to tell you the truth, I was having a few friends in tomorrow, just a couple of tables of bridge—"

"I'm sorry. I'll call him back," Catherine said, genuinely contrite.

"No, no. You want to go and we want you to do whatever you will enjoy. The little bridge party can easily be taken care of. But now, I hope you won't mind if I talk to you like an old Dutch uncle." She frowned at the desk top, then looked up abruptly. "Don't lose your head over César Saavedra. There, I can't say it any plainer than that. We've all heard of the shipboard romance, the case in which two people fall in love just because they are thrown together for a short time. They know it can't last. They know that soon they will have to return to their own worlds, so they fall head over heels into an intense relationship, to make up for lost time. And sometimes, in the most unfortunate cases, only one of the pair becomes emotionally involved. The end is not pleasant for that person."

"I know all that," Catherine said, reigning in her annoyance at Violet's assumptions.

"Oh dear, you're going to be angry and I can't say that I blame you. You think I'm a meddling old woman. But I feel I know you very well from all that María Lucía has told me about you. You're serious and sensitive and true, just the kind of girl to get hurt by

88

casual attentions because you don't take things lightly. Am I right?"

Catherine ducked her head to hide her emotions. She was, after all, touched by Violet's concern, and the words hit uncomfortably close to home. "Yes," she said finally. "However, I think this visit is really at the request of César's sister. I understand she is lonely for company, and I practically invited myself to go and cheer her up."

"Oh, well," said Violet, as if that explained everything. "By all means go. I would if I were you. But César Saavedra is no fresh-faced youth. I just don't want—"

"I know, I know," Catherine nodded. "You're right, and I'll be careful."

It was not until she was back in her own room that she wondered why it should seem so unlikely to Violet that César should simply like Catherine for herself. Surely even in Colombia, where social behavior was carefully watched, two people could meet and enjoy each other's company without causing alarm. No doubt Violet felt responsible for Catherine and hesitated to let her go out with someone she knew only by reputation. She herself didn't even know that much about César. Still, nothing could dispel her gay mood. She turned back to her correspondence and the morning flew by.

"The bullfights are one of the highlights of the sugar cane festival, along with the *cabalgata,* or parade of horsemen, and the crowning of a queen," Eduardo reminded Catherine a few hours later as the family settled themselves in the car. As they rode, Catherine could feel the excitement in the air, setting the orange blossoms of the acacia-lined boulevards aquiver and intoxicating the crowds that streamed toward the bullring. By the time they were in sight of the arena, traffic had slowed to a dusty crawl. Señor Imbert had to settle for a parking space a distance from the entrance. As they were walking across the parking lot, they passed roving vendors carrying trays of cigarettes, chewing gum, roasted corn, fresh fruit slices, and candy. The greasy, spicy smell of roasting sausages rose from crude grills near the entrance. Shouts and laughter filled the air. María Lucía's father bought several cones of brown paper full of fresh peanuts, and Catherine purchased some chewing gum from a gamin who followed her the length of the lot, wheedling and cajoling in a way that was at once impertinent and charming.

Their seats were halfway up the shady side of the stadium, which formed a steeper, deeper bowl than the ones Catherine was used to. She sat between María Lucía and Eduardo, who undertook to explain the intricacies of the age-old sport.

"I hope you enjoy it," he cautioned midway through his capsule history of bullfighting, "but if it disturbs you, just say so. Many people who have not grown up watching bullfights become upset."

Catherine was never to forget the thrill of the next moment, when a trumpet fanfare split the air, the main gate swung slowly and inexorably open, and a procession entered the arena.

"Three o'clock," Eduardo commented. "The bullfight is the only event in Colombia that starts on time. Listen—the band always plays a *pasodoble* to begin. Take these." He handed her a pair of binoculars. "The girl on horseback in the lead will have been chosen for her appearance, her ability to ride, and probably her family. It is a great honor to be chosen. Next come the bailiffs in ancient costume. The president will give them the keys to the bullpens, a symbolic gesture. Then you see each matador, followed by his retinue.

There are three matadors and each will fight two bulls."

Spellbound, Catherine scrutinized each in turn. The girl leading the procession wore her glossy black hair pulled back under a flat-brimmed black hat set at a rakish angle. A close-fitting bolero jacket, white shirt, black riding skirt, and boots completed her attire. Behind the mounted bailiffs stalked the three matadors abreast. Eduardo called her attention to each item of their dress: the "suit of lights," a tight-fitting jacket and kneepants heavily encrusted with gold and silver embroidery; pink silk stockings; flat-heeled pumps; and the traditional chenille hat, called the *montera*. Each carried a heavy dress cape of embroidered satin.

Catherine noticed one matador in particular. Although he was young, she thought he had the prideful, knowing look of a man who had gambled with fate and won, but who knew that the odds were never good. One would age quickly in such a profession, she imagined. The other two bullfighters looked considerably older. One received the hearty applause due a native son. Behind each principal matador marched the junior matadors, then the banderilleros, carrying the barbed staves, or banderillas, which they would stick into the shoulders of the bulls. Then came the mounted picadors with their lances. At the end came the gaily decorated mule teams, which would drag out the carcasses. Catherine listened to Eduardo's enumerations as she watched the bailiffs halt before the president's box. When the president leaned down to hand them the keys, the crowd sent up a roar. By that ceremonial act, the afternoon's sport officially began. The bailiffs galloped to the gate where the bulls would enter, holding the keys aloft, and the members of the procession progressed to their various posts.

"Isn't it grand?" María Lucía exclaimed. "My heart always beats faster when the music starts. Peanuts?"

"Yes, thank you." Catherine took a handful and adjusted the floppy straw hat Violet had lent her so that it shaded her eyes more effectively. The spectacle was almost too rich to absorb. She ranged her binoculars over the distant, sunny side of the stadium, where the cheaper seats were, then around the coveted box seats at ringside, which seemed to be filled to overflowing with dignified-looking gentlemen and magnolia-skinned women wearing elaborate coiffures. The kettledrums rolled. Trumpets rang out again and she swung the glasses back to the arena in time to see the first bull shoot into the ring like a black bullet. A deafening roar went up from the crowd as the bull raced around the ring, veering in a cloud of dust when its attention was attracted by a man with a cape.

Eduardo quickly informed her, "One of the subordinates will lead the bull through a series of prescribed passes with the cape. That is so that the matador can observe how the bull charges—whether he hooks to the right or left, whether he holds his head up or down, and so forth."

The ring held everyone's attention now. María Lucía's father sat forward, his lips parted in a half-smile. At the sound of the trumpet the subordinate retired and the senior matador began his preliminary capework, also to size up the bull.

"This fellow is from Mexico," commented Eduardo after a bit. "He rose very, very fast by taking big risks. You will see later what I mean. Next will come the picadors. Don't be afraid for the horses. Nowadays they wear thick padding. The purpose of the picadors is to get the bull to lower its head when it charges."

Catherine could not help wincing as the bull charged man and horse. The picador wore metal plates on his legs and the horse, too, was well protected. However, as the bull hit the picador's lance for the first time, the horse skidded backward and was nearly overturned. How long this combat lasted Catherine was not sure, for she used her binoculars to look elsewhere. Occasionally she turned them back to the ring so that the Imberts would not be disappointed, but she could not bear to look for long at a time. It seemed to her that any moment the strength of the picador or of the horse might fail, the lance be pushed aside, and the bull be upon them. She watched a scuffle among some spectators below them, and then María Lucía was telling her, "Each bullfight is divided into thirds. Now comes the second third, that of the banderilleros. The last is the most important one, when the matador and bull finally confront each other. It is called the *faena*. At the end of the *faena* it is time for the kill. You have probably heard the expression 'the moment of truth,' which is used to describe it."

The picadors had gone. In their place a man with two colored sticks—the banderillas—stood poised some distance from the bull. Suddenly, as the bull began his charge, the man sprang with balletic grace toward the bull, approaching from an angle, plunged the barbed banderillas into the shoulders of the bull, and sped away. The crowd roared its approval and Eduardo nodded, "Yes, a good placement." When three pairs of banderillas had been placed, the trumpet sounded for the last time. The moment of truth was nearly at hand.

The matador carried a short red cape. Catherine had noticed earlier that the heavy ceremonial capes had been spread over the railings of certain boxes and hung down the side of the ring. When the matador held up his hat in one hand, it was explained to Catherine that he was requesting formal permission from the president to kill the bull. Then he dedicated the bull to someone in the stands, threw his hat to the honored one, and turned back to the work at hand. The man began with several fluid passes that were linked together in such a way as to form a kind of dance. Around his slim body the red cape swirled now like a flag, now like a skirt, and seemed able to make the bull do its will. But soon the man threw caution to the winds. Catherine could not keep from clutching Eduardo's sleeve whenever the matador turned his back on the bull to walk haughtily away from him, or when he stood so close that his midriff was brushed by the bull as it passed. The music had a manic gaiety now and at each pass of the cape, the crowd shouted with one voice.

Violet leaned across her daughter to ask Catherine, "How do you like it? Are you all right?"

Catherine swallowed. "Fine, I'm just fine." She was almost relieved when at last the light sword that the matador had held under his cape was exchanged for a heavier one. "He will get the bull into just the right position now," Eduardo said. And then it was over so quickly that Catherine was hardly sure she had seen it. In sudden silence the matador and bull stood motionless opposite each other. Then the man lunged forward, the sword went in, and the bull collapsed with a convulsive kick. The crowd went completely wild. All over the stadium people waved white handkerchiefs and joined in a chant.

"What's happening? What do the handkerchiefs mean?" Catherine asked María Lucía.

"It is a sign of approval," she replied. "The people think he should be given an ear of the bull for his performance. In the case of an unusually fine performance, the matador may be given both ears and the tail; but I have never been lucky enough to see it happen."

The bullfight was a spectacle unsurpassed for either

beauty or barbarity, Catherine thought shortly afterward as the matador circled the ring, triumphantly holding up the ear he had been awarded, which had been cut off by one of his company. Even though she knew that it was probably the reaction of a neophyte, Catherine felt a twinge of sadness at the sight of the bull's carcass being dragged out by a mule team, making way for the next contest. By now she had deduced that even the slightest action of the participants carried a meaning, so completely ritualized had the sport become over the centuries. So, after seeing the matador hand the ear to a pretty girl in one of the boxes, she asked Eduardo, "I suppose he gives the ear as a special mark of favor? To a girl friend perhaps?"

"Yes, it is an honor to receive it from him."

"And what about the embroidered capes, the dress ones that are being displayed down there from some of the boxes?"

Eduardo took a look through his binoculars. "They are given to friends or sometimes to one of the ranches which supplies the bulls. Yes, I see that one to the right which is hanging from the box of Señor de las Casas. He is a very well known breeder. That was his daughter, Eugenia, who led the way into the ring."

Catherine focused her glasses on the group of people who sat in the box of the De las Casas. Eugenia de las Casas had removed the cordovan hat and her face was clearly visible. She was very beautiful, very aristocratic-looking, Catherine thought, with large dark eyes and full lips. Her straight nose and upright bearing would have given her a regal look, but at the moment she appeared to be laughing uproariously at something her companion was saying.

Catherine stared, gripping the binoculars so tightly that her hand began to cramp. Shock passed over her like trailing, icy fingers. Unable to tear her eyes away, she watched Eugenia de las Casas laughing with César Saavedra. His arm lay along the back of Eugenia's chair and his head was inclined toward hers to share the joke. They made a handsome couple, one had to admit. A man behind César tapped him on the shoulder and added something to the conversation, causing fresh laughter all around. Eugenia looked up adoringly at César, as if she had never seen anyone so clever.

Catherine was remembering her telephone conversation with César earlier in the day. How casually he had mentioned that he had to come into the city that morning! When she had told him that she would be at the bullfight, he had not said a word about his own plans to attend. A sense of betrayal welled up, nearly choking her.

The second bull had entered the ring, so the people she was watching stopped talking and paid close attention to the action. César alone sat back, relaxed, and his profile had about it the grave majesty Catherine had already come to associate with his name. From far outside it, Catherine looked down into the charmed circle of César's world and recognized her own feelings for what they were. Even as late as that morning, when Violet had warned her against falling in love with him, she had believed she was in no danger. How it had happened, that wrenching change, she did not know. Perhaps the surprise of seeing him just then, so near and yet so far away, had been the catalyst that forced her to call her emotions by their rightful name. At least she knew that she had never felt that way about Alex. As the first shock wore off and she grew calmer, she also knew that César had not betrayed her, because there was nothing to betray. Against all advice and common sense she had fallen in love with a man for whom she could be little more than a mild diversion. Her place was not there, amidst the wealthy ranchers and society beauties; it never had been and never would be.

The masses were screaming at some happening in the bullring; Catherine did not know or care what it was. Dimly she was aware that the situation exposed an appalling self-centeredness. A man was risking his life in the ring and she could not even pay attention. During the ensuing lull the faintest glimmer of hope made her turn to Eduardo and say with apparent disinterest, "I believe that is the man who gave me a ride from the airport, down there with the daughter of Señor de las Casas. They . . . look very happy together."

Reluctant to miss anything in the ring, Eduardo looked quickly and said, "Oh, yes, they're written up in the society columns now and again. Eugenia is quite a catch for him—and he for her, I'd say."

Catherine lowered her glasses and sat staring straight ahead. Some things were becoming clear. When they had been lunching at the country club, César had waved at some family friends but had declined to introduce her to them, saying that she would be bored. More than likely, though, it had been the other way around. César had undoubtedly felt that Catherine would bore the friends, or that she was unsuitable to be presented to them. Perhaps he had even been embarrassed to be seen with her. But, she continued to argue with herself, he apparently thought she was good enough to meet his sister. What was she going to do about tomorrow's visit? And why had no one told her about Eugenia before now?

Suddenly she felt that she had to get away and be by herself. The tightly packed bodies, the shouts and music, the dusty afternoon itself, were all pressing down, suffocating her. She half-stood, in order to look for an exit. She would just go for a walk outside and return in a few minutes; maybe she would feel better with a little fresh air. But the stairways to the exits had vanished: people were sitting on them. There was no way out. In the ring, the young matador slipped and fell, nearly under the hooves of the bull, and dropped his cape. The bull wheeled on him, but an attendant jumped out and distracted him until the bullfighter could scramble up, his jacket ripped by a horn. In the stands pandemonium had broken out. With her nerves already shaken, Catherine imagined that the crowd was screaming for blood.

"Are you all right? You're so pale!" María Lucía was shouting into her ear.

"What is it? What is it?" Violet called, adding in an aside to her husband, "I was afraid of this. She's going to be ill."

All of the Imberts were staring at her and Catherine was afraid that she was going to cry. "It's all right," she insisted, fighting for control. "Please, I—"

"You will come with me." The voice of authority belonged to shy, retiring don Carlos.

"I'll come too," María Lucía offered, gathering up her things.

"You will stay with your mother," he ordered as he held out a hand to Catherine.

Don Carlos made a path open in the sea of bodies, as if by magic. Catherine stumbled numbly after him. Somehow the second bull had been dispatched, although not in a manner that was pleasing to the crowd. All around her people were whistling, shouting, and stamping their disapproval, and Catherine could almost imagine that it was she instead of the bullfighter who was being cast out in disgrace.

The hall inside the stadium was unexpectedly cool and breezy. Carlos Imbert walked silently beside her, his hands behind his back and his face discreetly averted. Let him think she had been upset by the bullfight, Catherine told herself; she would die of shame if they knew the real cause. For a few brief moments she nearly forgot it herself as she concentrated on stilling the sobs that even yet swelled in her throat and threatened to break forth.

After several minutes they paused at the head of the ramp that led to the ground level. Señor Imbert handed Catherine a capacious handkerchief. "With my wife it was the same way," he said gently. "Just after I bring her to Colombia, so young, I take her to a bullfight. She is very, very disturbed, just like you. But now she enjoys it, after so many years." His eyes twinkled. "You see, I kept on taking her to them anyway."

Catherine managed a tremulous smile and felt a bit sorry about deceiving him. She said, "I know you don't want to miss any more of the *corrida*. María Lucía told me that the bullfights only take place once a year. Let's go back."

"Not until you have recovered. Not at all unless you do."

"But you can't miss it. I really believe I can go back now. It's just that it all came as a surprise," Catherine said, grimly aware of her double meaning.

When at last, much to Señor Imbert's relief, they were once more in their seats, Catherine assured the others, "I feel so much better, really I do. I just needed to get away from the excitement for a few minutes and have a breath of fresh air."

"I'm sorry it happened," María Lucía said, patting Catherine's arm. "We usually sit down closer to the arena but my father got these seats just so you wouldn't be able to see too well. In the box seats, for instance, you see the blood wounds so clearly—"

"That was thoughtful of your father," Catherine said fervently, her eyes straying once again toward the box of the De las Casas family. How much worse it would have been, she realized, to be sitting where César might see her, and where she would be tortured by every glance that passed between him and Eugenia. Now she understood how María Lucía must feel, looking on helplessly as Frank Gibson went his own way; and she was heartily sorry for any pain she might have caused her friend.

When Eduardo offered her the field glasses again, she said, "Thank you, but I'll just watch this way for a while." She could not help looking at César every so often, but at least he and his companions blended in an indistinct blur. Only once was she tempted to stare, and that was when she saw Eugenia and César rise. Apparently they had decided to leave early, for they were shaking hands and waving to friends nearby. Even at that distance Catherine saw the policeman who leaped to clear the aisle for them and the way in which the crowd parted, as if for royalty. She could not quell a pang of jealousy as she remembered the airport, where it had been she whose arm César had held so solicitously and she for whom the path was smoothed.

Yet as the afternoon wore on, with the cause of her pain no longer present, Catherine regained enough composure not only to watch and learn a little about bullfighting, but also to admit to herself what a fool she had been. Violet Imbert's description of the shipboard romance had been apt. Because Catherine was away from familiar places and faces, she had lost all sense of proportion and had refused to face facts. She, who had always kept such a tight rein on herself, had let freedom go to her head. When it was time to go home and Catherine stood up, she discovered that she felt weak and hollow, as if she really had been ill. *Being in love—or merely infatuated,* she thought wryly—*is like having the flu. When it takes hold of you, it possesses you completely and you can't think of anything else;*

but when it's gone, it's gone. Once during the evening, as she and María Lucía chatted and listened to music, she dully pictured César and Eugenia dancing and laughing together at one of the many parties of the holiday season, but she refused to let the vision linger. After tomorrow, she promised herself, she could and she would forget him forever.

CHAPTER SIX

The road to Palmira unrolled before them, hot and dusty. Catherine looked at the back of Leonardo's neck and wondered how many times he had driven Eugenia de las Casas over the same distance. The night before she had nearly phoned César to tell him she wasn't coming; only the thought of his lonely sister had made her reconsider. She had spent a restless night, full of gloomy dreams, but by ten o'clock, when Leonardo arrived, she was composed and ready. Uncertain as to what sort of day awaited her, she put on a sunbacked dress but stuffed a T-shirt and jeans into her shoulder bag. The Imberts waved her off with good grace, although Violet gave her a sharp look as she went out the door.

Catherine shifted her gaze to the flat pastureland through which they were speeding and continued a lecture she had been giving herself earlier that morning. She told herself sternly that she had arrived in Colombia the day after Christmas (and how far away Christmas seemed, in spite of the tree in the Imberts' living room and the strings of lights in the parks of Cali). It was now December thirty-first, hardly a week later, and certainly not enough time to come to a serious decision about anything. She ought to thank Eugenia de las Casas, in fact, for saving her from the excesses of a hopeless, spur-of-the-moment infatuation.

Because she had seen César and Eugenia together at the bullfight, today she would behave with a proper reserve. Her head was clear as a bell, even too clear, for she was thinking how convenient she and Alex had been for each other and how much they took each other for granted. Before Christmas, for example, Alex had told her that he wanted her to give him a particular set of tools and even where they could be bought. She had dutifully purchased them and had given them to him unwrapped, because he had remarked how ridiculous it would be to pretend that he didn't know what he was getting from her that Christmas. For his part, he had given her a bottle of her favorite perfume exactly like the bottle he had given her for her birthday. Oh, it was dull, dull, with no surprises and no romance. Did life have to be that way? Was it ungrateful to want more? Alex would never make her unhappy. But what she was asking herself for the first time was whether or not he would be able to make her really happy.

Leonardo was threading his way through the streets of old Palmira, at scarcely more than a walking pace, between whitewashed walls aslant with age, and Catherine glimpsed one of the many horse-drawn carriages that still operated as public conveyances in that city. What automobiles there were, were ancient— César's Mercedes seeming to be the sole exception— and she felt as if she were slowly sinking back into an earlier, simpler time.

She tried to resume the frank talk she was giving herself to put both César and Alex in their proper perspectives, but one wayward thought kept returning and interrupting the lecture: How was she to deny what she had felt with César? In spite of their arguments and the way he had put her on the defensive, something had passed between them, a spark of understanding, a connection that had seemed strong enough to build on. She had been certain that he had felt them, too, those moments when everything seemed bathed in a mellow light and there was no yesterday or tomorrow. She sat up straighter. No, people did not live without yesterdays and tomorrows. Her head must rule her heart, and no faltering.

They turned left down a side street, which gradually widened the farther it went from the center of town and at last became a rutted dirt road. For half an hour they bounced past fields of sugar cane, with Catherine breathing shallowly to avoid taking in any more dust than she had to, until Leonardo stopped before a wooden gate flanked by two square stone columns. He got out and laboriously dragged the gate aside, drove through, and closed it behind them. Once through the gate, they crossed a swirling, muddy river by means of a rickety bridge and entered a tree-lined avenue. The trunks of the trees were thick and gnarled with age and the tops spread a deep shade.

Leonardo spoke for the first time since they had started. "Señorita Gray, there it is, Los Limonares."

Through the trees Catherine saw the house, an imposing sweep of stucco and red tile. The central portion was two stories high and was flanked by two one-story wings, the whole being unified by a veranda that ran across the entire front and appeared to bend around the sides as well. While the house stood in full sunlight, the lawn was shaded by more of the ancient trees, under which two horses cropped grass. To one side stood a square stone building surmounted by a steeple. The little chapel appeared, if anything, even older than the house, and in disrepair. Unpretentiously, almost crudely constructed of materials native to the region, the house commanded attention for its enormous age, its size, and for the way it seemed to have evolved naturally out of the landscape. It was, Catherine saw at once, a place that had seen births and deaths, hard work and happy times, marriages and wars, countless partings and homecomings. It was a monument to the history of the Saavedra family. She could not but feel at once honored and humbled to be invited inside its doors.

Leonardo swung the car in a wide arc around the lawn and pulled up before the steps to the veranda. As Catherine stepped out César strode through the open door of the house to meet her. He looked quite different from the dapper traveler and guide she had seen before, dressed as he was in an open-necked shirt, riding pants, and dusty riding boots. His face was flushed and the wind had ruffled his hair. Catherine was struck as never before by the contrast between the touch of gray at his temples and his taut, youthful face.

"Welcome to Los Limonares." He took both her hands in his and looked into her eyes with genuine pleasure.

"Thank you. I'm very impressed," Catherine responded, taking in the house and grounds with a sweep of her arm.

"And I am flattered. I know that you are not easily impressed." He winked. "I apologize for being dressed this way but there were problems with one of the tractors and I just got in from the fields. There is always something to see to. Come, Isabel is waiting in the patio."

They walked down a cool hall that led straight through the house and onto a roofed patio, where lawn

105

furniture and potted geraniums mixed casually. Just outside the low railing that bordered the patio grew carefully tended bushes of hibiscus and camellias. Farther beyond, Catherine could see the grove of lemon trees that gave the hacienda its name.

At their approach the girl in the wheelchair turned from staring into the trees. To Catherine's surprise she had ash-blond hair, which she wore pinned in a heavy coil at the nape of her neck, and the palest of skins. Her brother had spoken the truth when he said she was beautiful, but her face had a pinched, tired look, which Catherine took to be the mark of an inactive life upon a spirited temperament. César went to stand by his sister, giving her an encouraging pat on the shoulder as he did so. "Well, here we are," he said. "Catherine, this is Isabel—"

"And Isabel, this is the famous Catherine," his sister finished, holding out her hand. "I am very glad to meet you."

"And I'm glad to meet you too," Catherine returned, wondering at the same time what César had told his sister about her.

"Tonight is New Year's Eve," Isabel said. "A good time for making new friends as well as for remembering old ones. César says you must be back in time for a party."

"Yes, I'm going with the Imberts, the family I'm visiting, to a New Year's dance at one of the clubs."

"Oh, yes, those club dances. . . ." Isabel trailed off wistfully. Catherine saw a shadow of pain pass over César's countenance.

A maid came in with coffee then. Catherine had noticed that the arrival of a guest in a Colombian household, no matter what the hour, always provided the occasion for a cup of the national beverage. César wheeled his sister over to a glass-topped table at the

106

edge of the patio, where the maid was setting out an exquisite demitasse service and a plate of bonbons.

"Maya! Here, miss, miss," Isabel called softly and a big black-and-white cat scrambled down from one of the lemon trees and bounded over to take its place in its mistress's lap. "This is my constant companion, my faithful Maya," Isabel explained to Catherine. "She never runs off, leaving me alone for days at a time, as some people do. Do you know, I had to spend Christmas Day by myself?"

"Why, of course," Catherine remembered, turning to César, "you were on the plane when I came down the day after Christmas."

César winced. "There were unusual circumstances and it couldn't be helped. You know that, Isabel. It won't ever happen again."

His sister pouted prettily as she held Maya up to her cheek. "Oh, I know, but it wasn't any fun."

"Remember, Aunt Florencia asked you to stay with them," César said gently.

"I don't like it at Aunt Florencia's," Isabel objected, a whining note creeping into her voice.

Instead of answering her, César said to Catherine, "You said you were going to the bullfight yesterday. What did you think of it?"

Catherine saw that César was trying to avert a family quarrel by changing the subject, but she would rather not have been reminded of her painful discovery of the previous day. "I'm afraid I can't judge," she stammered. "It's very beautiful, but at the same time cruel, I should say. I wonder why it has quite the enormous appeal it does in some countries and for some people. Señor Imbert is going nearly every day." She did not want to tell him or have him discover that she could hardly remember a thing that happened in the ring after the moment when she had seen him with Eugenia. She would try to keep the conversation general.

César leaned back in his chair and shoved his hands into his pockets. "A great deal has been written and said about bullfighting," he said easily. "Some say that the bullring is the last place in the modern world where one man alone can confront the dark forces of the universe, which of course are represented by the bull. Then, too, Latins admire courage enormously. Some people even claim that you must understand the bullfight in order to understand the Spanish soul. I was there yesterday, by the way. I thought the bulls were very good."

"Well, I think the bullfights are boring," Isabel burst out. "The same old thing time after time. Tell me something new, Catherine. What are the fashions for spring? We are so isolated here."

Catherine did her best to oblige the girl by speaking at length of the latest clothes she had seen advertised before Christmas, as well as of recent books and records. César looked on indulgently, the creases in his brow relaxing as Isabel became more animated and cheerful. Once she abandoned her initial irritability, a ready wit and lively curiosity shone through. Catherine found it easy to forgive Isabel's manner but suspected that it would be hard on César to have his sister so dependent on him and so jealous of his time. They talked pleasantly until the sun had passed its zenith and the shade of the lemon trees had taken on an underwater density. When lunch was announced, Isabel promptly broke off the conversation, shooed the cat from her lap, and they all went inside to the dining room.

The interior of Los Limonares possessed an austere beauty, with its lofty ceilings and smooth floors of stone and tile. The furniture was massive, old, and in need of refurbishing. Catherine thought, as Frank

Gibson would say, that it needed a woman's touch. As the three of them sat down at the dining table for twelve, which filled the center of the oblong dining room, she guessed that if the sun-faded draperies were replaced and the walls painted, the room, with its arched entrances, would be magnificent. Cream walls instead of gray would be nice, with a thin, brick-red stripe in the draperies to pick up the color of the floor tiles. The empty brass bowl on the sideboard was made to hold flowers, lots of them. The chandelier of wrought iron looked as if it had once held candles but had since been wired for electricity.

"A penny for your thoughts, that's the expression, isn't it?" César said as the maid slipped plates of soup in front of them.

Catherine started and reached for the damask napkin beside her plate. "I—I was just thinking what a lovely room this is. The proportions are grand."

César nodded. "Yes, my mother used to love it. That is her portrait behind you. Since she died, my father has turned over Los Limonares to me and spends most of his time in Bogotá."

Catherine turned to admire the oil painting on the end wall. It showed a fine-boned woman in a sapphire blue dress, seated beside a table on which stood a vase of camellias. Catherine glanced from the painting to Isabel and back again. "You look like your mother," she remarked, noting the similarly rounded features. "But you and César are as different as night and day."

Isabel smiled and put a hand to her hair, obviously pleased at the attention. "César looks like the other side of the family, the fierce ones. Did he tell you about Grandfather Saavedra, the one who became a general when he was twenty-one?" With that she launched into a string of colorful anecdotes about the early Saavedras. It was a shame, thought Catherine as

109

she listened, that such a skillful storyteller should have shut herself away from people. Genuinely interested, she questioned Isabel, thus calling forth further reminiscences and legends, so that the discussion lasted the length of the meal. When they had finished and the last of the china and heavy silver had been removed from the table, César spoke up. He had been listening for the most part and had contributed little to the conversation.

"I would like to take you on a tour," he said to Catherine. "Can you ride a horse?"

"Not well, but I won't fall off," Catherine answered. "I even brought some jeans."

Isabel threw her napkin down and said petulantly, "There you go again, taking Catherine off so you can have her all to yourself. And what am I supposed to do in the meantime?"

César gave his sister a straight look but his voice was mild. "I imagine you will lie down as you always do at this time. We won't be long."

"We don't have to go. I'll be glad to stay here if Isabel wants company," Catherine put in.

"That won't be necessary," César said as he continued to look steadily at his sister. "Isabel, when we come back, we'll take you down to the river. Would you like that?"

Isabel said to Catherine in a disparaging tone, "He's always making deals like that with me, as if I were a child. All right, I'll have my nap. The maid will show you where you can change."

When Catherine came out onto the veranda in her shirt and jeans a few minutes later, César had saddled the two grazing horses.

"You take this one," he said, leading the palomino mare over to her. "She is gentle." He helped Catherine mount, then swung up on the big bay he called Alazán.

110

"We'd better not get too far away from the house," he added. "I don't like the way the sky looks." They went around the south wing of the house, past the outbuildings, and started down a dirt road that led into a sea of sugar cane.

"You haven't told me my horse's name," Catherine reminded César.

César looked at her out of the corner of his eye and a slow smile spread across his face. "I thought you would never ask. She's called La Potranca."

"*Potranca?* I don't remember that word. What does it mean?"

César chuckled. "The colt."

"Oh!" Catherine began to laugh. "You planned it, didn't you?"

"Well, I will have to admit that when I thought about which horses to saddle up today, there was only one possible choice for you, Little Colt." After a moment he added, "I tamed that one, you know. La Potranca was given to me when I was a boy."

"Oh, yes, I've heard that you tame colts," Catherine said lightly. She felt miles away from the nervous girl on Cristo Rey, sure of herself and emotionally uninvolved.

The air had become heavy and still. Even the birds had ceased their twitter. The only sound was the clipclop of the horses and the rhythmic swish of the machetes of the cane cutters. *"Buenos días, don César!"* called the ones nearest the road and César touched the brim of his straw hat each time in acknowledgment. They passed wagons being loaded with bundles of cane and a worker told César that the tractor was running properly again.

"I would have been glad to stay with Isabel," Catherine reiterated as they jogged along. "She seemed disappointed when we left."

111

"You saw something of her petty side," César said. "I'm sorry."

"Don't apologize. I think she's very nice," Catherine hastened to say. "She just wanted attention and the children I teach have made me used to that. I only wonder if we shouldn't have stayed with her. After all, you invited me here for her benefit."

"You are not enjoying yourself."

"Oh, I am!" Catherine exclaimed. "But if I am supposed to be entertaining Isabel, why, then I ought to do it."

They had slowed the horses to a walk so that they could talk. César said quietly, "Isabel was only showing off a bit for you, take my word for it. It is true that I was gone on Christmas Day, but she accepted the circumstances at the time. And I am sure she does not begrudge me this hour. You leave the day after tomorrow, no?"

"Yes, I do."

"Perhaps next New Year's Eve, when you and your husband are seeing the new year in, you will stop for a moment and think about this day. . . ."

Catherine bent her head. He would never know just how much she would think about today, the last time she would ever see him. She took a deep breath and said, "I suppose you have plans for this evening too? New Year's Eve seems quite special here."

César shrugged. "Yes, there are plans." As he seemed disinclined to discuss them, Catherine assumed that they concerned Eugenia and that César, quite rightly, saw no reason to share them with her. Instead he began to speak of the plantation and the methods for growing and processing cane. When they came to the river, which described a large curve through his property and formed part of its eastern boundary, César pondered the muddy waters a moment before remarking, "I don't understand it. The water is usually much clearer. It might have been stirred up by rains upstream, but this is not the rainy season." He scanned the horizon, where dark clouds were massing. The wind had freshened and could be heard singing in the cane.

"Yes, we'd better turn back," César decided at last. "Down there, where that spit of land juts out, we used to swim when we were children. My brother, Julio, and I used to have races to the other shore, fighting across the current. It can be swift." His face softened with memories and they lingered silently for some time, watching the water swirl savagely around the rocks.

"And Julio, where is he now?" Catherine finally asked.

"Julio runs the export end of the family business in Bogotá. We don't see each other much, but we are still close. He is between Isabel and me in age. He wanted to get away from here and live in the capital from the time he was old enough to think about a career. He likes to be able to advise government officials about trade and to be close to the decision-making places. But I"—he turned in the saddle to survey the gently rolling fields—"I wanted to stay close to the land. Our people have always belonged to the land as much as the land has belonged to them. I hope it shall always be so."

Catherine watched him as he sat erect, facing into the wind. She wanted to tell him that she understood, that his love for the soil spoke to something deep within her, but she could not find the words and she dared not disturb the moment with chatter. All too soon he sighed and, turning his horse with a gentle pressure of the knee, led the way back. They rode more and more briskly, for the sky had taken on a dirty, yellowish-gray cast and the trees bent like suppli-

113

ants before the wind. "We didn't see the horses and cattle," César shouted, "but the next time—" The wind whipped away the rest of his words.

Catherine held on and tried to remember all she knew about sitting a horse, hoping she didn't look too foolish, for she had never had formal training in riding. César must have forgotten that this was her first and last trip to Los Limonares when he had mentioned a next time, she thought, though how could he have forgotten when only minutes before they were discussing her departure? Then they were clattering through the gates to the fields and up to the stables, which were some distance behind the house. César dismounted quickly, threw the reins to a stable boy, and came over to Catherine. "Jump," he ordered, smiling at her.

As she started to dismount he caught her around the waist and set her gently on the ground. Catherine looked up at him, awed by his nearness, and just then fat drops of rain spattered them. César grabbed her hand and they began to run, the shock of the rain causing them to burst out laughing. By the time they gained the corner of the veranda, they were drenched and gasping for breath. Still laughing, exhilarated, with hands still clasped, they leaned against the wall and watched the rain come down in sheets. Out of the corner of her eye Catherine saw a dark shape move in the doorway and she touched César on the sleeve. He looked toward the door.

"What is it, Rosario?" he asked.

A squat woman with deep-set eyes stepped out of the shadows. "I came to look at the sky," she said. "It is going to be very bad, don César."

"Rosario is our cook," César explained. "Rosario, this is the Señorita Gray. Rosario knows many things. Tell us, just how bad is it going to be?"

The woman shook her head somberly. "Maybe as

bad as in the time of don José. It will be a very, very bad storm."

"How can you tell?" asked Catherine.

Rosario looked at her haughtily, as if she were not sure whether the question deserved an answer. "I know," she replied and melted back into the shadows.

"Rosario is quite a character," César mused. "She was born at Los Limonares and pretty much has the run of the place. She claims to see signs others don't, and she is right often enough to make one pay attention to her. The other storm she mentioned happened almost sixty years ago, but people still talk about it. There was a flood and the water got up to the top steps of the patio."

"Let's hope she's wrong," Catherine said. "Do you know," she went on, "I had my palm read last Sunday. I was told that I was searching for something, that I don't yet know what it is, and that I would not see my home again for a long time. What do you think of that?"

César looked at her and then away. "Miracles do happen," he remarked. "Maybe someday I will tell you about one that happened to me."

Catherine quickly drew her hand away from César's when she heard a voice say, "Back early?" and Isabel came out onto the gallery.

"I'm afraid you don't get your ride down to the river today," César told her.

"What is it they say in the States? I'll take a 'rain check.' " Isabel laughed, apparently over her annoyance at being left alone. Nevertheless, the glance she shot at Catherine was coolly appraising.

César turned back to Catherine. "We need to change clothes, don't we? I wouldn't want to take the blame for sending you home ill. And you, too, Isabel, should be inside."

Catherine went to Isabel's room to slip back into her dress. The sound of the rain had swelled to a roar, drowning out all the household sounds. Somewhere outside she heard shouts and went to the window. Isabel's room was in the back of the house and Catherine saw that the shouts and screeches came from two young servant girls who were trying to get some clothes unpinned from a clothesline to the left of the lemon grove. The storm had evidently taken the whole plantation completely by surprise.

Although the room had grown very dark, Catherine did not turn on a light. Did César's voice have a peculiar tone whenever he mentioned her going home, or was her imagination supplying the emphasis? Would he remember her at all in a year?

As she continued to look out the window and daydream, César dashed across an open space and entered one of the buildings below the house. Moments later he emerged with a coil of rope slung over one shoulder. A worker followed him out and they set off together for the fields.

When they first met, Catherine had thought him one of the idle rich; but to see him at Los Limonares was to see a different man.

Catherine finished dressing and went over to Isabel's vanity table to brush out her damp hair. A number of photographs and newspaper clippings, some yellowed and curled, ringed the glass. Several showed Isabel in riding costume, and in one she was receiving a trophy. Catherine concentrated on a group of family snapshots. One, taken in front of Los Limonares, must have been the whole family several years back. Isabel was not among them, so presumably she had held the camera. Catherine recognized their mother from the portrait in the dining room; and the gentleman beside her, a taller, more severe version of César, must be the father. Julio,

César's brother, would be the heavy-set young man with glasses standing in front.

Catherine tried to guess how many years ago the photograph had been taken, for César looked considerably younger and more carefree. Ten, perhaps. Who was the girl beside him? A cousin? A sun hat shaded her face so that the features were barely distinguishable. Catherine scanned the other pictures quickly, aware that Isabel would be wondering why she was taking so long. She did not see Eugenia de las Casas in any of the informal shots, although the girl in the hat appeared once more.

The sound of a piano, muffled by the rain, led Catherine to Isabel. She found her in a formal living room full of dark and ancient furniture, playing a rosewood piano. Without missing a note or turning around, Isabel asked, "Do you sing?"

"I can try," Catherine replied, moving to stand behind Isabel. The girl was playing from a book of ballads. Catherine did not know the song being played, so she began by humming tentatively. Since they were alone, she sang out on the next song and soon was following the melodies with pleasure. From time to time she ventured a glance at Isabel, anxious to know if she was relieving the tedium of the day for her. It was hard to say, for the face under the golden hair was a mask of concentration. She wanted Isabel to like her, but she fancied that it was not easy to win approval from any of the Saavedras.

They went on and on. Once Isabel stopped to ask, "Can you do harmony?"

"I did a little in the chorus when I was in school," Catherine answered. "You take the melody and I'll try to fill in the alto."

"No need to keep standing," Isabel said in an expressionless voice. "Sit down."

117

Taking the invitation as a mark of favor, Catherine pulled up the piano bench, which had been turned aside to make room for Isabel's wheelchair. They began anew, going more slowly.

Night falls suddenly in the tropics and that afternoon the roaring curtain of rain hastened its arrival. After a time Catherine found that in spite of the floor lamp by the piano, she had to lean forward to read the words. They sat isolated in a circle of light. Occasionally a crack of lightning electrified the air, causing the room to reconstitute itself suddenly and then to disappear again just as precipitately. Each time the thunder followed closer.

"So this is a tropical storm," Catherine said between songs. "It takes one's breath away, doesn't it? I've never been in anything like it."

"Neither have I," Isabel returned carelessly as she smoothed down the next page.

As it happened, they were singing "La Paloma," a song Catherine knew well, when, with a deafening crackle and clap of thunder, the lights went out. Isabel's fingers faltered only slightly, her voice not at all. Over the sound of their singing they heard screams and scurrying feet in the direction of the kitchen. Doors opened and shut; someone bumped into something and laughed. Then the voices settled down into small exclamations of satisfaction as, no doubt, candles and matches were found. Just as they finished the song a doorway brightened and César stood there, drenched to the skin, holding a blazing candelabrum. In the moment it took him to cross the room, Isabel turned slightly in the darkness and murmured not so much to Catherine as to herself, "Mmmm, you'll do." Before Catherine had a chance to think what she meant by it, César was saying to her, "It looks as if you'll be stay-

118

ing the night. The bridge to the Palmira road has been washed out. I'm sorry."

"You don't look sorry," Isabel observed tartly. Her brother favored her with another of his long stares but said nothing.

"There is only the one road?" Catherine inquired.

"No, there is also the dirt road we took with the horses; but even if it were passable, it would take a long time to get back to a highway. An automobile couldn't make it over the ruts, especially in the mud. You see, it is a wagon trail. You'll miss your party tonight."

"I don't mind, really I don't," Catherine said. "But I should telephone the Imberts and let them know what has happened."

"But that's impossible. We don't have a telephone," Isabel chimed in.

Catherine looked from one to the other in surprise.

"We don't need one except when my father is here," César explained, "and that isn't often. His duties as a senator keep him in Bogotá most of the time. And I use our house in Cali for business. So you see, when you come to Los Limonares, you leave all the problems of the outside world behind."

"It certainly seems that way," Catherine agreed as she looked at the way the candlelight polished his bronzed face. What she did not say was that to come to Los Limonares was also to enter a field of force created by César himself. Those hallmarks of character with which she already was familiar, the strength tinged with melancholy, the austerity shot through with humor, were palpable in every room and over the broad fields. To come to Los Limonares was to submit to his personality. She had been fighting such a submission, but she felt her will weakening. Now even the elements were conspiring against her, imprisoning her within the magic circle of his life.

"But what about the lights? What happened to them?" Isabel was saying.

"Something is wrong with the generator," her brother answered. "I sent the mechanic to see about it and I'm waiting for him to report. Rosario was right, it looks as if we're in for a bad night. I've never seen the river flood so quickly. It had to be caused by a cloudburst in the mountains, coupled with the thunderstorm here."

César left the candelabrum with them and went away. Catherine accompanied Isabel to confer with the servants about meals and about opening one of the spare bedrooms for her. Isabel's mood swung rapidly from friendly acceptance of Catherine's presence to clumsily veiled resentment. It was strange, Catherine thought, that a stranger's visit should affect Isabel so. She must have lost her ability to deal easily with people after her injury.

Because César was busy monitoring the progress of the storm and its effect on Los Limonares, the three did not reassemble until just before nine o'clock, when dinner was to be served. As the air had grown damp and clammy, Isabel lent Catherine a powder-blue shawl and draped a white one about herself. Catherine received the soft woolen wrap with relief, for the darkness and the strain of coping with Isabel's mercurial temperament had begun to tell; she felt cold and tired.

They were served cocktails in the formal living room. The light from thick white candles, which had been placed at intervals around the walls, softened the heavy lines of the furniture and made Catherine think of the firelight in her grandparents' house when she was a child.

"I thought we could offer you a pleasant, uneventful day in the country, but perhaps, after all, crisis is more our style, more typical of the way we live," César said to Catherine as they sipped their drinks. They were seated in two matching armchairs, facing each other over a marble-topped table. The candle on a stand at César's elbow threw half of his face into relief, highlighting the crescent-shaped scar on his cheek. Just then he must look, Catherine thought, like the "fierce" side of the family. Isabel had asked to be placed at some distance, near a brace of candles, so that she could sort some sheet music. Rain still lashed the windows. Although the lightning had ceased, the wind seemed to be steadily gathering strength.

"Is there any danger? To the house, I mean," Catherine wondered out loud.

César chose not to answer. Instead, he swirled the ice in his glass and said, "Candlelight becomes you."

"You didn't answer my question," Catherine parried.

"You didn't accept my compliment."

"Thank you," Catherine said awkwardly. "Now, is there any danger?"

"To the house? Possibly. To the inhabitants? Almost certainly. To some of them, that is."

Catherine looked up warily. A pulse began beating in her throat like terrified wings. "Am I included in the inhabitants?"

In the flickering candlelight he looked like a panther waiting to spring. "Did I ever mention," he said offhandedly, "that the blood of the conquistadors runs in our veins? The Saavedras', I mean?"

"I'm not surprised," Catherine remarked, in a faint attempt at sarcasm.

"The conquistadors," he went on almost dreamily, holding his glass up so that the light turned the liquid to glowing amber. "There is much to be said against them. But they were persistent and they nearly always got what they wanted. We have, I suppose, gotten used to that over the years, getting what we want."

"Render unto César the things that are César's," murmured Catherine.

"That is very good, yes," he smiled. "We don't mind challenges, of course."

"But first you have to know what it is that you want," Catherine said, her voice almost a whisper. "Do you?"

"Do *you*?"

The maid found them staring fixedly at one another in the gloom when she came to announce that dinner was served but that the Señorita Isabel would be eating in her room.

"But is she ill?" Catherine asked, turning to look at the spot where Isabel had been, realizing that she must have gone out the door across the room without their noticing.

"She says she is only tired, señorita, and that she will join you after dinner," the maid replied.

"We should have been paying more attention to her," Catherine exclaimed, exasperated with herself.

"I spoke with Isabel this afternoon. I'm sure she is all right," César said cryptically. "Shall we go in to dinner?"

As they took their seats, Catherine glanced up again at the portrait of César's mother, which glimmered silver in the candlelight.

"Do you like camellias? They were her favorite flower," César said, following her gaze.

"Why, I don't know. They're such a rarity where I live," Catherine replied. "I've never seen more than one or two at a time, in corsages."

"How dull to live in a place where such things are a luxury," he teased.

"We have other flowers just as pretty, I daresay. But I did see something unusual the other day," said Catherine. She told him about the bus heaped with purple flowers that she and the Imberts had seen on the way to Frank Gibson's.

César nodded. "You have caught the paradox of Colombia in that image. The rickety bus is the poverty and the backwardness that always accompanies our progress; but the flowers, those are the beauty of the land and the people."

Miraculously a full dinner had been prepared without electricity. Once César was called away from the table for a long time and came back looking worried. Otherwise the meal was peaceful and Catherine lost some of the strange elation she had felt during their conversation before dinner. They both talked easily of growing up and of their families, although once or twice Catherine received the impression that César stopped short of telling her something important. At eleven thirty, when they had finished their coffee and Isabel still hadn't come, César suggested, "Let's go to my sister's room. We can bring her back here or I'll have something sent there so that we can toast the New Year."

Walking close together, in the circle of light thrown by a kerosene lamp that César carried, they made their way down the long hall. When several knocks at Isabel's door produced no answer, César gently turned the knob and they looked in. The light from a guttering candle fell on Isabel's hair, which was spread on the pillow and itself lit up that corner of the room, as a single shaft of sunlight transfigures a forest glade. The book she had been reading had fallen to one side and a dinner tray, scarcely touched, lay at the foot of the bed.

"Poor child," César whispered. Leaving the lantern

with Catherine, he crossed the room on tiptoe. He removed the book and tray, pulled a blanket up over the sleeping girl, and blew out the candle. "We won't wake her," he said when he returned. "She doesn't sleep well and any rest she gets is to the good."

As he pulled Isabel's door shut, a dull, splitting noise reached them from outside. Glancing at his watch, César said, "If you don't mind, I think I will wish you a happy New Year a few minutes early. I had better go find out what that was."

"No, go ahead," Catherine urged. "They fixed up the room next to Isabel's for me so I'll just say good night. I'm usually asleep by this time anyway."

All at once there seemed to be nothing to say. In the wavering lantern light César looked steadily down at Catherine and she felt as if she were drowning in his black eyes. "You said that some of us might be in danger," Catherine stammered, her mouth suddenly dry. "What is the danger to you?"

He reached out and very gently touched her cheek. "You keep the lantern," he said, and disappeared down the dark corridor.

CHAPTER SEVEN

Catherine shut the door to her room behind her and leaned against it. Out of the storm-tossed night César's face still looked down on her, the message in his eyes unmistakable. He needed her. Of that she was as certain as if he had told her in so many words. Had he asked her then to stay at Los Limonares, she would have consented without hesitation. His look, in fact, had asked her. But how she was to reconcile that message with what she knew of his life and with the responsibilities of her own, she could not fathom.

There was Isabel's conduct to baffle her as well, the erratic behavior during the day followed by the silent withdrawal before dinner. Isabel seemed to be testing Catherine, but to what end? It was all very mysterious, she thought as she lifted the kerosene lantern so that she could examine her sleeping quarters. Would that she could throw light on the enigmatic Saavedras so easily.

The room was sparsely furnished and obviously not in general use. A massive mahogany armoire, an iron bed with a nightstand beside it, an old sheepskin rug, dark blue curtains, and a chaise longue of the previous century completed the décor. Catherine tried the light switch but the generator apparently had not yet been repaired. When she crossed to the bed, she saw that a long, white nightgown of cotton plissé, undoubtedly one of Isabel's, had been laid out for her. The lacework edging the neck and sleeves had been done by hand, a detail that strengthened Catherine's notion of Los Limonares as an anachronism, a charming remnant of colonial days. On the nightstand stood a blue earthenware bowl brimming with camellias. Beside it rested a hand bell of tarnished silver. Catherine set down the lantern and lifted the flowers to her face, breathing in the heady fragrance. César must have given the order to place them there while he was away from the dinner table. She was surprised and flattered that he would have attended to such a detail in the midst of more pressing matters.

With the bowl of flowers still in hand, she pulled the curtains back from one of the two windows in the room and sat down on the window seat beneath it. Because the rain was beating full upon the panes, she could discern nothing outside. It was nice being alone with the rain. She drew up her knees and rested her back against the embrasure. The Imberts would be worried about her, especially if they knew the precise path of the storm, but she hoped that they had gone to the party without her. She would rather be where she was.

Bowing her head from time to time to drink in the scent of the camellias, she let her mind wander back to other New Year's Eves. No one made much of the holiday back home: the year before, as they always did, her father had gone to bed at his usual time, while she and her mother had waited up until midnight. They each wrote predictions for the coming year and placed

126

them in sealed envelopes, to be opened the next New Year's Eve. Neither of them, of course, had foretold that Catherine would be in South America when it was time to open the envelopes.

When she thought about it, in fact, the idea of visiting María Lucía had jelled surprisingly fast. Invited many times before, she had never seriously considered making the trip until three weeks before this Christmas. No wonder Alex had been so alarmed. Her decision had been almost an act of desperation. One day, as she supervised the children at recess, she had suddenly seen her life trudging by, in a patient lock-step, with nary a deviation to the right or left. Probably the vision had been brought on by her discovery, the evening before, of her first gray hair. It was premature, to be sure, but it had sent a chill down her spine nevertheless. That afternoon after school she had visited a travel agency. From there she had gone straight home to write María Lucía and tell her she was coming. Only then had she told Alex.

Well, that decision was past and she was enjoying the consequences. She closed her eyes and tried to see her mother sitting in the kitchen. She wondered if her mother was opening their predictions of last year and what new ones she might be composing. She herself would not dare to guess what the New Year would bring, except that she felt in her bones that her life would never be quite the same as it had been before her trip. She was changing, waking up to thoughts and feelings that were new. The year before last, she remembered, she and Alex had gone to a party for the employees of the store where he worked. They had left immediately after midnight and one cup of punch, because Alex was an early riser. And the year before that . . .

The sound was faint but unmistakable. Somewhere

127

in the dark and sleeping house an old-fashioned key-wound clock was chiming the hour of midnight. "Happy New Year," Catherine whispered to the creamy petals, and stopped to listen again. If the event was being marked by anyone else at Los Limonares, she could detect no evidence of it. Only the soughing of the wind met her ears. She thought that she ought to make a resolution, but she could think of nothing she wanted to accomplish that was in her power to effect. Fatigue settled down on her then, like a wet, gray fog, and she arose to get ready for bed. She did not even bother to wash her face. Within five minutes she was curled up in the iron bed, the lamp extinguished; and within six she was asleep.

Some hours later, morning light, fish-belly white, seeped around the blue curtains to awaken her. She had slept heavily, dreamlessly; being awake was only a slight change from her sleeping state, for her body lay like a dead weight across the mattress and her mind hovered somewhere above her, a distant blank. She dozed, awoke, and dozed again. It wasn't the light, but rather some noise that kept waking her. She rolled over and raised herself on one elbow, sweeping her hair out of her eyes with the other hand. Isabel's voice and that of someone else cut sharply in on each other just outside her door.

"—But I tell you, I do not know how long, señorita," the other voice insisted. "All I know is that his bed has not been slept in."

"Then we will have to wake her," Isabel said. "She may know when he left."

A rap at the door sent Catherine scurrying across the room. "Is anything wrong?" she asked as she opened the door wide to allow old Rosario, the cook, to push Isabel's chair into the room.

"It's César," Isabel said, her voice tight and high. "He didn't come down to breakfast at the usual time and Rosario says he's not in the house. She thinks he may be . . . outside, in the . . . Do you know anything?"

"We came to your room just before midnight, but you were asleep," Catherine explained, trying to think clearly. "Then we heard a kind of cracking noise outside and César went to see what it was. I didn't see him after that."

"You didn't hear him come in?" Isabel asked.

"No, I went to bed in a few minutes and then went straight to sleep." Catherine found herself in the unpleasant position of being an intruder upon a family crisis. Although Isabel was dressed, her hair hung in tangles and she plucked distractedly at the fur of Maya, who crouched in her lap. It was obvious that she, too, found Catherine's presence awkward, and she was struggling to appear calm.

Catherine broke the silence. "But couldn't he just be busy somewhere? At the stables?"

"If the señorita would look out the window—" volunteered Rosario. "It's as I said."

Catherine did so, then turned back open-mouthed. Isabel nodded grimly. "Yes, we're on an island. The house is completely cut off from the other buildings. Who knows how deep it is farther out."

"Has anyone been to look for your brother?" Catherine asked. "Some of the field-workers, for instance?"

Isabel shook her head. "No, it's still so early and we've only just discovered he's gone. I suppose I should send someone over to the workers' quarters. . . ." Suddenly her eyes filled with tears and she slammed her fist down on the arm of her wheelchair. "Oh, I'm so helpless!"

"Look, I'll just get dressed and then I can . . . well, help somehow, do something. Maybe I could go," Catherine offered.

"Don César is all right," the cook assured Isabel as she turned the chair toward the door. "By the time you've had breakfast, you'll see, he will be back." But her face, which Isabel could not see, remained stern and worried.

As soon as they were out of sight Catherine hurriedly dressed in pants and a shirt and went out onto the veranda. The world had changed since she had stood there laughing with César the afternoon before. Then she had not realized that the house, quite fortunately, stood on a slight rise, which now lifted it inches above the milk-and-coffee-colored ocean that stretched in all directions. One of the fine old trees in front of the house had split nearly in two at the cleft. That had probably made the noise César had gone to investigate.

Catherine walked the length of the veranda, which bent around the house and thus afforded a view on three sides. The stables and other outbuildings stood to the right and back of the house. Directly behind the house, she knew, lay the lemon grove. To the left and back, at some distance, were the workers' quarters; she saw them indistinctly beyond a line of trees. César might be seeing to the generator, wherever that was, or he might be looking after the livestock. She remembered that the evening before he had mentioned that he had horses and cattle somewhere on the property, and that they would have to be moved if the water rose. Perhaps there was a barn she hadn't seen.

At any rate, the storm was certainly over, she assured herself. The sky was a cloudless, faded blue and the wind blew cool and steady, but not hard. At the moment it seemed ridiculously simple to Catherine to remove her shoes, roll up her pants, and step into the water. She would just wade out a little way from the house to see what she could see.

The cold water made her shiver. In the back of her mind played horrid scenarios in which César was hit by a falling limb during the storm, electrocuted by live wires in the water, knocked unconscious and drowned by a frightened animal he was trying to save. They played over and over, varying gruesomely. She decided to go to the north, or left, of the house, toward the workers' quarters, thinking that it was more likely she would find someone in that direction who might have seen César.

Near the house, the water came up to her knees and the grass of the lawn made slippery going. A little farther on some splintered boards floating against a tree trunk indicated to her that real damage to property had occurred. By the time she reached the line of saplings that screened the workers' quarters from the rest of the plantation, the water had risen to her waist and the effort necessary to walk was beginning to tire her. The sun was well up by then and the warm, cloying smell of wet earth rose from the flooded land.

Through an open door in one end of the long building, she saw the flotsam of daily life bobbing disconsolately in the dirty water. Later, much later, it was suggested to Catherine that she should have turned around and gone back to the house then; that she should have reasoned that if no one was in the workers' quarters and if César was not in the house, then they all might be together; that, in fact, she should have done almost anything but what she did do. But the building offered a definite destination, and in any case Catherine was not thinking of herself. She stood in the empty landscape and considered only one fact: César was missing. In all the distance she had walked, she had seen no trace of him. She decided to go on to the building, just in case someone was there, and then, after a look on the other side of it, go back to the house. If he hadn't turned up by then, she could try the other direction after she had rested and reported to Isabel.

The sun beat on the crown of Catherine's head and she had to shield her eyes from the glare on the water to see any distance at all. Her scrutiny of the scene was careful. Time and again her nerves jumped as she fancied that some dark object projecting from the water had a human form. Once she was startled by a fluttering from above, which turned out to be three bedraggled chickens roosting in a tree.

She had traveled perhaps twenty yards farther toward the building and had just noticed what seemed to be a current moving across her path, when the ground gave way sharply and left her treading water. She was not afraid, for she knew how to swim. But it did begin to dawn on her how little business she had wandering over unfamiliar terrain in the middle of a flood. She was convinced of it moments later when a snake slid past her shoulder, its sinister head undulating as it swam. Suddenly the water was filled with unnameable horrors and she imagined that something cold and filmy had touched the back of her neck.

A recurring nightmare of her childhood, in which she floundered in a deep pool, the edges of which receded each time she approached them, was suddenly coming to life. Catherine struck out, away from the snake. That was enough to send her into the current, which she had forgotten about. Surprised at its force, she tried to swim out of it, but without nearby landmarks she had no sense of direction. The river, she knew, was not here, but rather on the other side of the plantation, so she concluded that she must have stumbled down the bank of a stream that fed into it.

She did not know the position of the workers' quarters in relation to the stream, but figured that the stream ran between them and the line of saplings. She tried to swim across the current, hoping she would soon run up on a bank. Every time she put her foot down, however, it met only with water. After a while it seemed to her that the building was farther away than it had been, so she turned on her back to rest and to try to think.

Inside her, an icy worm of panic began uncoiling. No one knew where she was. It could be hours before anyone tried to look for her and she could not stay afloat for hours. She was not that strong. She wished that she had at least eaten breakfast, so that she would have more ready energy. As had happened in other times of stress, a sentence from her voracious reading of magazines appeared to bedevil her. This time it was, *The average human head weighs fifteen pounds.* Hers seemed to be growing heavier and heavier as she labored to keep it above water. The sentence kept repeating itself. Something rough struck her leg but she could not see what it was in the opaque water; her knee stung as if the flesh had been broken. Again she tried to swim to each side, searching for footing, but she soon gave it up as a waste of energy. A great distance away she saw a file of trees that might be the tree-lined avenue leading to Los Limonares. If so, then she would be swept into the main river, which surely was more treacherous and swift than the stream she was in.

"Help! Someone help me!" she screamed, tears blinding her, but the surrounding silence blotted her voice and reduced it to a cricket chirp. She beat her arms wildly and swallowed a mouthful of water before she could regain control of herself. After that she forced herself to swim a modified breaststroke with her

133

head up, so that she could watch for help or for something to hold on to. When she tired of that, she switched to a sidestroke, then finally relapsed into alternately floating on her back and treading water. It was as she was changing from her back to an upright position that she was thrown against something hard, a searing pain shot through her skull, and she lost consciousness.

She was out only for a few seconds, then came up coughing. Her lungs burned from the intake of water and pinpoints of light danced before her eyes like maddened fireflies. Blindly she thrashed about and as she did so, her hand hit something solid. Instinctively she circled it with her arms and hung on. As she continued to gasp and shudder, she felt the water eddy around her. She was no longer moving.

Catherine looked up blearily. A shattered railing sloped into the water from above her, one end still attached to a post high up. It took her a minute to realize that she had been carried onto the wreckage of the bridge that led to Los Limonares, the bridge over which she had arrived the day before. That meant that if she could only get up the bank somehow, she could probably make it back to the house by walking or swimming down the avenue of trees. But just then she was so tired, and the ache at the back of her head was so numbing, that she continued to cling feebly to the remains of the bridge, her head in the crook of one arm. It did not require much effort, for the rushing water kept her pushed against the boards.

Later it was estimated that Catherine might have been under the bridge for as much as an hour, but at the time it seemed to her that she had just put her head down for a few seconds, intending to rest a moment before trying to find a foothold, when she was half-roused by shouts. Then someone splashed into the water quite close to her and her arms were being pulled away from the post. She did not like that and she tried to get loose from whoever was bothering her, but strong hands and arms lifted her away inexorably and at last she gave up the struggle. Someone said, "She's hurt, be careful," and then she saw men and horses with the water not so deep, just up to the horses' bellies.

"Can you stand up? Do you think you can sit on a horse?"

"I . . . was . . . looking for you," Catherine said weakly to César, who had one arm around her, holding her up.

"We'll try it," he said curtly to someone near at hand. "Take her now and then hand her up to me."

Then she was sitting in front of César on the big horse called Alazán (she remembered the name clearly) and his arms encircled her, holding the reins and keeping her from falling. But she nearly did fall off twice, so little control did she have over her body; and each time he gripped her more tightly and whispered in her ear, "Steady, steady, I'm going to take care of you, don't worry, it's only a little farther now."

Just when she thought she could not sit up another minute, Isabel, old Rosario, and two maids came into view on the veranda, screaming and exclaiming. The horses stopped.

"Where have you been? What's happened to Catherine?" cried Isabel.

"I thought you would know what happened to Catherine. We found her down near the bridge. If she hadn't been stopped by it, she would have been swept into the river. I took the men over to help the Fernandezes. They sent word last night that they needed help. Raúl, stand here to get the señorita down."

Pure pride raised Catherine's head then and made

135

her say, "I can get down by myself. Please step aside. I'm fine." All at once, as she moved to dismount, the dancing points of light returned before her eyes. Then, like a flock of homing pigeons, they converged toward one spot until there was only that one point of light. When that bright spark flicked out, she was in darkness.

When next she opened her eyes, she was alone in the room in which she had spent the night. Sunlight slanted through the long blue curtains and blue shadows waved in the corners of the room. Catherine raised her head from the pillow and rapidly let it fall back as a cloud of pain swirled around her. When she gingerly raised her hand to the back of her skull, her fingers encountered a bandage that caused the whole ordeal to come back to her. She rested her hand at her side again and looked about the room. She had some memory of old Rosario and a maid turning her this way and that. It must have been they who had stripped off her wet garments and put her back in the plissé nightgown. After that there had been some treatment, with the sting of alcohol cutting across the other pain. She remembered giving someone a long description of her trials, only to discover at the end that she had been thinking it all to herself and hadn't uttered a word.

Moving cautiously, Catherine raised herself on both elbows and from there eased herself up to a sitting position. She leaned her pillow against the headboard of the bed and lay back against it, panting from the effort. Her hands were scratched front and back, and her right knee throbbed dully. Drawing the covers aside briefly, she saw a bruise and swelling above the kneecap. Across the room the doorknob twisted noiselessly and Isabel rolled herself into the room.

"Oh, you're awake. How do you feel?" she asked.

"I'm not sure yet," Catherine confessed. "I've just been taking an inventory of my wounds."

Isabel cocked her head to one side and gave Catherine a questioning look. "I don't understand what you were doing. I expected to see you in the dining room for breakfast. When you didn't come, I sent Rosario to your room. We had no idea where you had gone. Imagine how I felt, with both you and my brother missing."

Catherine sighed. "I know you think I'm an idiot and I guess I am. I really only meant to wade out a little way from the house. But the farther I got, the more I felt like going just a bit farther. I think I must have fallen into a stream. It carried me down to the bridge."

"Maya is always doing something like that," Isabel remarked. "Her curiosity leads her to get stuck in the most unexpected places. César says that we ought to have one servant who does nothing but follow Maya around and rescue her." Then she added quietly, "You were worried about César, weren't you? That's why you did it."

After a moment's hesitation Catherine admitted that it was.

"We were both foolish," Isabel said, "foolish as only women can be. I shouldn't have jumped to conclusions when he wasn't in the house this morning and of course you shouldn't have acted upon my conclusions. But when it's a question of the safety of someone you care for, prudence is unthinkable." She said it easily, naturally, as if it were something she and Catherine had discussed and agreed upon many times before. Although Isabel had come to scold, Catherine now felt that she had changed her mind and might even be proposing a kind of alliance between them.

"But I feel so embarrassed. You have enough problems without my making a fool—and a burden—of myself," Catherine said. "I will never be able to live this down."

"I can see how you would feel that way, but don't forget that I am as much to blame as you are. Besides," Isabel continued, "what if something really had happened to César? Then you might have made the difference between his being alive and—Catherine, are you all right?"

When she had first sat up in bed, Catherine had felt the first tremors of a chill coming on. Now her teeth had begun to chatter and she huddled miserably into the bedcovers, unable to control her shaking.

"I'll see that more blankets are brought and have Rosario make some hot broth for you," Isabel promised, wheeling her chair around and starting for the door.

Catherine pushed herself to a prone position, closed her eyes, and gave in to the trembling, which gradually escalated into racking shudders. She slid into a half-stupor in which, after a while, she was barely aware that someone was spreading more covers over her. Nor did she open her eyes when the cup of broth was set on the table beside her; not, that is, until an arm slipped under her shoulders, raising her slightly, and César's voice said, "Drink this." Obediently she drank from the steaming cup, her teeth clicking crazily on its rim. She choked once and he sat down on the edge of the bed and raised her a bit more to help her swallow. Then he carefully tucked the covers under her chin and let her head lie back again, cautioning, "A little at a time, but be sure you drink it all. Rosario's broth will cure any ailment known to man."

"I'm sorry," Catherine stammered.

"Sorry?" he said gently. "Don't be sorry."

"I'm sorry for all the trouble I've caused," Catherine maintained as she struggled to raise her head.

"Careful," César admonished her. He helped her to another sip of broth. "You've had a mild concussion, you know. The rest is just exhaustion and shock, but a concussion is something to reckon with."

After a bit Catherine asked, "Did you lose any livestock? And the cane—is it bad?"

"Bad enough," he returned soberly. "But don't think about that now. Don't think about anything except getting better. You had a narrow escape."

"But I want to tell you something."

"I know," he said, "and I will tell you something. But not now. There is so much time."

She wanted to tell him anyway and to ask him why there was so much time, but she was very tired just then and was content to sip the broth when it was offered. She did not remember finishing the cup, however, nor did she know when he left the room. When she woke up again, it was dark save for a lamp burning in a far corner of the room. Beside it, in a straight-backed chair, sat a girl Catherine had not seen before, dressed in a maid's white uniform. She was stocky, with straight black hair and a flat, serene face.

"I see the generator has been fixed," Catherine said, feeling she ought to say something.

"Yes, señorita."

"Are you—supposed to stay here?"

"Yes, señorita. Don César told me to stay."

"But I don't need anybody. I'm much better." She sat up and found that she indeed was. "Look," she said, swinging her legs to the floor and standing up. Proudly she took a half-turn around the room before returning to lie down. Immediately she knew it had been a rash move and hoped the girl hadn't seen how close she came to fainting. As if Catherine were a

139

child, the girl ignored the demonstration and continued to sit, her eyes calmly gazing somewhere over Catherine's head. After a little while, as Catherine was carefully shifting to one side, she slipped out of the room. In a few minutes she returned to resume her vigil.

I want to tell you something. She had said that to César before she went to sleep. She couldn't remember what she had wanted to say, though it had seemed urgent at the time. And he had said something back to her, but what? If it had not been for the chills, which were gone, and her exhaustion, which was not, where would the conversation have led? She had not been herself and she might have said—admitted—something she would regret. How fortunate, then, that it had gone no further.

"I haven't been talking in my sleep, have I?" she said, suddenly worried.

"No, señorita."

Still, it had been good to have him there beside her, so gentle and concerned. She had felt safe.

Outside, someone ran his fingers across the strings of a guitar once, twice, then stopped to adjust the tuning. A song began, sung by four or five voices and accompanied by a seductive rhythm on the guitar.

"What is that?" Catherine asked the girl, raising herself on one elbow.

"It's a serenade. Don César told some of the men they could sing if you became better. I went to tell them that you might enjoy a few songs."

"You mean it's for me? Then I must get up."

The girl came forward shyly. "With your permission, señorita, I will explain the custom here. When a girl receives a serenade, she must not show herself at the window. However, she should give a sign that she is listening. She can turn a light on if the room is dark or move the curtains or, in this case, turn the light off

140

briefly." She stopped, then added timidly, "It has been a long time since we had a serenade at Los Limonares."

"You have been working here a good while?" Catherine inquired.

"All my life, señorita. My mother is the cook."

"Then you are the daughter of Rosario," Catherine said, fancying she could see something of the cook's square and solemn features in the daughter. "You are right to assume that I know nothing of the customs of your country. Do you mean to say that serenades are not performed often?"

"Oh, no," the girl replied. "They are special. Don César has not given a serenade since—" She broke off, raising a hand nervously to her lips.

"Since when?" Catherine prodded.

"Since—I was a young girl," she finished.

"Perhaps you should signal now with the light," Catherine suggested. She suspected that the girl was holding something back, but was at a loss as to how she might extract the information from her. "What's your name?"

"Arcelia, señorita," the girl answered. Her face had closed up as if she were afraid of something. She turned off the lamp momentarily, then turned it on again. Returning to the bedside, she asked, "You still have pain?"

"Only when I laugh," Catherine joked, but Arcelia remained serious. With scrupulous care she measured some pills into her palm and poured water into a glass on the nightstand. "Don César says you must take these," she said.

"They're so big. What are they for?" Catherine asked.

"They are for the pain, of course," Arcelia explained as she helped Catherine to drink.

141

"I just wanted to make sure they weren't sleeping pills," Catherine said. "Don't tell the musicians, but I can hardly keep my eyes open."

Arcelia went back to her chair in the corner. With each breath Catherine drew, she could smell the bowl of camellias. It seemed ages since she had first taken the bowl in her hands, instead of only twenty-four hours. Even time was different in Colombia, more elastic and somehow less measurable.

Outside, the men were singing a sad song about an acacia tree and how it reminded a man of his lost love. Years ago he had sat with her beneath the tree. Now she was gone and he stood under it alone, remembering his former happiness. Catherine wanted to cry for the poor man in the song. Was the girl dead or had she gone away with another? Had the words a special significance for her situation or was it just another song? It was hard to concentrate on the words with her head throbbing. How much easier just to close her eyes and feel herself surrounded by the scent of the flowers and by the music, surrounded by the attentions of César.

CHAPTER EIGHT

"What do you think you're doing? You are forbidden to get out of bed!" At the sound of a step behind him, César had turned from the scattered papers on the patio table. Catherine, fully dressed, swayed in the doorway. As she took another faltering step forward he leaped to her side and guided her to a chair beside his. "I'm only letting you sit here a moment to rest," he warned her, "and then back you go."

Catherine curled forward to rest her head on her knees. When the dizziness was gone, she sat up again and said, "But I can't. Do you know what day this is? Do you know where I'm supposed to be right now?"

"Suppose you tell me." He was stroking his mustache absently, watching her.

"At the airport! This is the day I was supposed to go home!"

"You look ghastly, you know."

"Thank you. Just what I wanted to hear," Catherine grumbled.

"You're very pale. Did you take the medicine this morning?" he asked.

"Yes, I took the medicine. Didn't you hear what I said?" Catherine asked testily.

"Something about the airport, I believe," César said with studied indifference. "A wonderful invention, the airplane, though not quite the indispensable machine some people would have one think."

"It doesn't bother you a bit that I missed my plane, does it?"

"No, I can't say that it does," he returned amiably. Then, suddenly serious, "I won't be glad to see you go."

Taken by surprise, Catherine looked away from his intense countenance. She made herself notice that the water had receded from around the house, leaving mud halfway up the trunks of the lemon trees. The flowering shrubs beside the patio had been robbed of their blossoms and stood bowed and broken like so many Cinderellas when, after the last stroke of midnight, they find themselves once again clothed in rags.

"But I can't stay here," she protested weakly. "What about the Imberts? What about my family? What about my job?" She felt stiff and sore, and her wits, she knew, were no match for César's that morning.

"I've already been out to inspect things this morning," he said, "and the water is down everywhere. I can send a man to telephone and let your hosts know that you are all right. Even though you really are not all right," he reminded her.

Catherine closed her eyes as another wave of vertigo passed over her. When she opened them again, César was still watching her gravely. Slowly he said, "My poor Catherine. Does it ache so very much?

"It comes and goes. And I feel so weak and cross with myself," Catherine admitted.

"How would you like to stay out here and get some fresh air?" César suggested. "I'll have a chaise longue

144

brought out and set over there in the shade. Since I'll be working on the payroll for a while, I can keep an eye on you and see that you don't go ambling over the countryside again."

Catherine made a face at his gibe but said, "All right. I'd rather not go back to bed if you think the doctor would allow me to stay up. I'm not feeling as strong as I was a few minutes ago."

"The doctor thinks it would be perfectly all right for you to remain here," César declared, his eyes twinkling.

"You——?" Catherine gasped.

"But of course, my dear," César said. He was enjoying himself enormously. "Who else could have done such a fine job of diagnosing and bandaging? Doctor Saavedra, at your service."

"I learn something new every day. I thought you were a lawyer, not a doctor," Catherine parried.

César shrugged. "I am whatever I need to be. There was no way to bring a doctor in time and I am used to treating the workers when they are injured. I intend to send for someone to have a look at you today, however. Now no more talking. You must rest."

In a matter of minutes Catherine was ensconced on the chaise longue, with extra pillows at her back and a light afghan tucked around her legs. Talking had made her short of breath and she was relieved just to sit quietly in a dreamy haze. Through half-closed eyelids she watched César at work. His face was partly turned away, so that his commanding profile presented itself. Twice, when she awoke from a doze, she found that he had turned to look at her pensively. At her glance, he merely smiled and went back to his papers. His foreman came once for a long consultation and once he went away for a time. From inside, in an unbroken flow, came the rippling notes of the Chopin études that

145

Isabel was practicing. Catherine experienced it all in a sun-dappled daze. The memory of her travel plans intruded occasionally, buzzing about like a bothersome insect, but for the most part she was content to put off decisions and rest. Once a doctor arrived and made a diagnosis, she told herself, she would begin to take charge of herself again. She was awakened for good, however, by the excited barking of a dog on the other side of the house. Sometime, somewhere, she had heard that same dog before, she was thinking, when something wet touched her hand and she jumped awake.

"Trapper?" Catherine exclaimed in astonishment.

César rose from his chair and fired her a questioning glance as, close upon the arrival of the dog, Frank Gibson strode through the hall entrance. The confrontation of the two men was a sight Catherine would remember for a long time, for it was like the meeting of two elemental forces, the one light and the other dark. Frank's voice boomed out, shattering the bucolic calm of the morning.

"Say, you must be César!" he exclaimed, pumping the other's hand vigorously. "I'm Frank Gibson, a friend of Catherine's, I guess you'd say, and I'll tell you! We've all been pretty worried back in town. Glad to see the house is still standing and you folks are all right."

César assumed an air of hauteur that would have frozen a lesser man, and even Frank seemed to hesitate, as if he were for an instant aware of himself as an interloper. By way of greeting, César merely inclined his head and said, "Mr. Gibson," hardly moving his lips. Much to Catherine's surprise, his behavior bore all the hallmarks of jealousy; and while she herself was annoyed at Frank's interruption of the precious time they were sharing, she had not dared to assume that

146

César would feel the same way. She wanted to tell him exactly who Frank was and that there was no cause for alarm, but at the same time she could not help but be pleased that her presence made a difference to him.

Meanwhile, Frank had recovered his momentary loss of composure and turned to inform Catherine, "I never saw such a mess—crops destroyed, animal carcasses caught in trees and fences, houses caved in. I had to leave the Land-Rover on the other side of that river, where the bridge is washed out, and walk the rest of the way. 'Fraid Trapper and I got ourselves pretty muddy." He shuffled his feet apologetically and patted Trapper's head.

Catherine, who had been silent since his arrival, said, "Land-Rover?" stupidly, for she could not quite comprehend the reason for Frank's presence.

"Not mine," Frank explained. "You know my old truck wouldn't make it over these muddy roads. No, Señor Imbert let me have one of the ones from his factory to come looking for you."

"Is it bad in the city? We've heard nothing," César inquired with formal politeness.

"Lots of roofs leaking and some slippage in one of the suburbs on the mountainside, but nothing like what you've had out here," Frank told him.

"Won't you sit down?" César asked, indicating a chair next to his.

"No, thanks just the same," Frank returned. "Actually, what I had in mind was to go right on back and take Catherine with me. She's already missed her plane, you know, and the Imberts will want to know how she is as soon as possible. I take it you weren't able to phone?"

"No, there is no telephone. However, I'm afraid it may be impossible for Catherine to be moved until she has seen a doctor."

"What?"

"She has . . . met with an accident," César said, obviously wishing to say as little as he could to Frank.

"What accident? What happened?" Frank wheeled to look at Catherine, his eyes widening as he saw for the first time her pallor and the way her hair had been fastened up to allow a compress to be placed on the back of her neck; but his question was directed to César. The latter added little to his original remark, saying only, "She's had a fall. A slight concussion is the worst of it."

"That settles it," Frank declared. "We've got to get her back to Cali to see a doctor. There must be a ford somewhere in the river, right? Tell me where it is, and I'll bring up the Land-Rover. You can't cure a concussion with home remedies."

Catherine saw a look of contempt flash across César's face as he heard his judgment impugned. He did not stop to argue the point, however, but restrained himself and reiterated that Catherine had to rest longer before making a trip.

How strange it was, Catherine mused, to lie weak and boneless as a jellyfish, listening to oneself being discussed as if one were not present at all. She was about to call attention to that fact when Isabel came onto the patio, her chair pushed by Arcelia, the maid who had stayed the night in Catherine's room. Frank softened his belligerent stance somewhat in deference to Isabel, but still seemed almost fiercely determined to carry Catherine off immediately. After Isabel had heard both sides of the issue, which were presented with palpable antagonism, she shrugged prettily and said, "I don't see what the problem is. You are not dealing with an unconscious patient. Catherine should be able to tell whether she feels well enough to go or not. Why don't you ask her?"

It was obviously a new idea to them and they both turned to look at Catherine. At that moment she had again been thinking to herself what a troublesome guest she had been for the Imberts. In addition to having upset their entertainment plans, she had allowed them to worry about her safety during the flood without sending word to them, so that they had had to ask Frank to search for her. Now there would be new travel plans to make and her convalescence to oversee. Because of all those reasons and because she thought it would also be more convenient for the Saavedras if she left with Frank, Catherine said bravely, "I'm feeling much better. I think I can go with Frank."

No sooner had the words left her mouth than the look on César's face told her she had made a grave mistake, and she wished she had not tried to be so selfless. A great deal more had been riding on her answer than she had supposed. In a flash of intuition, she realized that, for him, the questions had not been whether or not she was able to travel, but rather whether she would entrust her care to him or to Frank, and whether she would respect his judgment or Frank's. She wanted to cry out that he was mistaken, that she had been thinking only of what was most convenient for everyone, and that, furthermore, the reason for Frank's insistence was his anxiety to please María Lucía.

Evidently César believed that Frank had come out of his own concern for Catherine, not at the behest of the Imberts. He must have imagined that there was something between them and that Catherine, by her choice, had ratified the relationship. But it was too late. He had turned to Frank and was discussing, very coolly and rationally, how to get the Land-Rover up to the house.

Catherine lay back miserably and let the logistics of

the removal and transportation of herself from Los Limonares be debated. She might as well be a load of sugar cane, she grumped to herself as she watched the two men. As he listened, Frank, in faded denim and muddy boots, ran his hamlike hand over Trapper's head. A lock of hair had fallen over César's brow, softening his face. He looked tired and worn, in spite of the aura of virility and physical toughness that always surrounded him, and Catherine belatedly remembered how much he must have had on his mind because of the destruction wreaked by the flood. Yet he had not said a word about his troubles, but had treated her as if her recovery were the problem of paramount importance at Los Limonares. It was part of his code, she supposed, to present a calm demeanor in the face of adversity.

She closed her eyes and then must have fallen briefly asleep, for she was startled by a low voice close to her ear saying, "It's time for you to go now. I'll help you to the car." César's cheek was close beside hers as he bent to slip an arm around her waist and raise her from her couch. As they walked slowly down the hall that led to the front of the house, she had to lean against him and let his strength serve for them both. When they came out onto the veranda, Frank was waiting in the Land-Rover with Trapper on the front seat beside him. Pillows had been placed in the backseat so that Catherine might comfortably recline during the ride.

Catherine took a couple of unsteady steps by herself to reach Isabel, who had held up her arms to embrace her. *"Hasta la vista, Catalina,"* Isabel whispered, and Catherine was both touched and perplexed by the intimate friendliness the girl showed by using the Spanish form of her name. *"Hasta la vista,"* Catherine returned, well aware that she was repeating not "good-bye" but "until we meet again." Then César turned her and guided her to the vehicle, where he got in with her to arrange the pillows and make sure she was comfortable. Neither had spoken, but, as Frank Gibson questioned one of the workers, who was cleaning up debris in front of the house, about an alternate route to Palmira, César took Catherine's hand. For a long moment, as he held it, they stared as if mesmerized into each other's eyes.

"Your hand is trembling," he said at last.

"So is yours."

He favored her with one of his brilliant smiles and gave her hand a squeeze, thus breaking the spell. "Good-bye, Catherine Gray. May you always have the last word," he said, and stepped out of the Land-Rover to return to the veranda.

"Okay, ready to roll," Frank shouted. "Nice to meet you folks!" They were on their way. Catherine looked back until the house was lost from view. Isabel remained outside, but César had turned on his heel and gone inside as soon as they started.

It was true. His hand, when closed around hers, had been possessed by a controlled tremor, as though a strong current passed through it. A phrase from Pascal that she had learned at school came to her: *We know the truth not only by the reason, but by the heart.* No matter what anyone said, no matter if heaven and earth appeared to disclaim it, the truth had reached her heart in those moments before they parted, and she could not deny what she felt and what she knew he felt. She lay back, exhausted with emotion.

Some time later Frank stopped the Land-Rover and went into a building to telephone the Imberts. They were making slow progress because of the mud and it would be a long while before they reached their destination. She dozed. When she opened her eyes again, they were moving. Frank saw in the rearview mirror that she was awake.

"How do you feel?" he asked.

"Lazy," Catherine smiled.

"I called the Imberts," he told her, "and they said they would have a doctor waiting when we arrived. You really had them worried, you know, so I guess they're just relieved you didn't drown."

"Frank," Catherine said slowly, "how did it happen that you were sent for me? Did they call all the way up to your house and make you come down to the city?"

"Not exactly," he said. "I was listening to the radio and I heard about the heavy rains hitting Cali. The newscast reported that some houses on the mountainside were already beginning to slide. It sounded to me like the Imberts' section of town, so I phoned. As it turned out, the report had been unclear and it was really the shanties to the north that were going; the better homes weren't affected at all. But María Lucía sounded so anxious about you on the phone that I went down to see what I could do to help."

The lightheadedness made Catherine reckless. She felt wise beyond her years and saw everything from a great distance, as if she were moving little toy people around on a board. She said, "I think you made a mistake when you stopped seeing María Lucía. You miss her, don't you?"

"That happened a long time ago," Frank temporized. The back of his neck turned beet-red.

"I've known María Lucía for a long time," Catherine said, abandoning the direct frontal attack. "She was one of the most popular girls at school, with both girls and boys. She had her pick of boyfriends and we all envied her invitations to private-school dances. Nothing like her social life would ever have happened to me."

"I can't believe that," Frank said gallantly.

"What I'm trying to say," Catherine persisted, "is that María Lucía has been admired all her life. She is good at socializing because first of all, she enjoys it and is naturally gregarious, and second, she's had a lot of experience. But that's not all of María Lucía."

"I know it isn't," Frank agreed.

"Ah, you know that," Catherine said on a note of triumph. "Then you know that she's not a frivolous person, not deep down. She's actually a very serious person in many ways. And practical. And loyal and—"

"You don't have to read me a lecture on María Lucía's virtues," Frank said a trifle huskily. "That wasn't the trouble at all, not from my point of view. I think the world of that girl."

"I was going to say, 'and she cares about you,'" Catherine finished.

Frank said nothing for a quarter of a mile. Then, awkwardly, he began, "I don't have much to offer a girl. Not that it got to that stage, you understand. But I got the feeling from her parents and Eduardo that I wasn't to come around very often."

"Did they say anything to you?"

"Not for a while. I guess they expected me to get the idea from their behavior or something, but I've got a pretty thick skin and I didn't take the hint. Finally her brother took me aside and gave me some song-and-dance about how I was restricting her freedom to meet other fellows and how I didn't exactly fit into their plans for her."

"So it was not the parents, but Eduardo, who warned you off," Catherine said.

"Right," nodded Frank. "In fact, I was surprised when I was invited to the party for you. I didn't think I was the type the Imberts wanted to show off to their guests."

"I wonder if Eduardo might not have been speaking only for himself. I have noticed that he is almost overprotective of her. If I remember correctly, Señor Imbert is largely a self-made man, and Violet—Mrs. Imbert—doesn't strike me as status-conscious. She is a law unto herself! They wouldn't stand in the way of María Lucía's wishes just because you don't belong to the right club. Could it be possible that you jumped to the wrong conclusion and so did María Lucía? Oh, her parents may have said something to her, but I wonder if Eduardo hasn't been deceiving you both. It's just a feeling I have and maybe there's nothing to it. What reason could he have, though?"

"Beats me," Frank shrugged. "But María Lucía didn't seem that sorry to see me go."

"Frank!" Catherine marshaled the last of her strength, determined to get her point across. "What did you expect her to do? Chase you down the street? She isn't the type and you know it." She added bluntly, "I'm really surprised you gave up so easily, a brave fellow like you."

"I think I'm as good as anybody, but I don't go where I'm not wanted," Frank declared.

"But you *are* wanted. You made María Lucía very unhappy when you stopped calling." Another thought struck her and she continued, "Do you suppose don Carlos would have lent you this Land-Rover and asked you to come out here if he disapproved of you? Would he have taken advantage of your kindness in such a way?"

"I guess not," Frank admitted. "So what am I supposed to do now, Miss Cupid?"

"To begin with, you can teach María Lucía how to handle Trapper." She took a deep breath and added, "And name a rose after her."

It hardly seemed possible that the back of Frank's neck could get any redder, but it did. In the heavy silence that followed, Catherine massaged her temples with the tips of her fingers. A dull throbbing had set in and in order to break its rhythm she pressed so hard that a red mist swam before her eyes. If only she were as skillful at managing her own affairs as she was at managing those of other people, she might still be with César; at the very least, she would not have a concussion. Now that she had had her say, she was surprised, even alarmed, by her own boldness. But Frank had tipped his hand when he had telephoned María Lucía during the storm to see if she was all right. He did care about her and, Catherine rationalized, what did it matter what he thought of her, Catherine, if her talk with him did some good. Eduardo's role in the affair was puzzling, however, and would have to be cleared up. As soon as she felt better, she resolved, she would try to find out whether or not he was the sole origin of the objections to Frank.

Cali did not look much different, except for the abundance of leaves and twigs strewn about by the winds. As they passed the rushing, foaming Río Cali, Catherine was reminded of her nightmarish hours in the water and she shuddered.

María Lucía and Violet hurried out to the street as soon as they arrived, getting in each other's way and contradicting each other's orders.

"Ladies, ladies, just stand to one side," Frank said indulgently, adding under his breath, "Flapping around like a couple of drunken butterflies." Somehow, in spite of all the help she received, Catherine was transferred to her room without jarring her head too much, and Dr. Pérez, a stocky man of about fifty with tinted spectacles and an ingratiating smile, undertook to assess her condition.

When he had finished his examination, Dr. Pérez called in Violet and María Lucía, who had been waiting anxiously in the hall. "Miss Gray has had the proper care," he announced pompously, "and now, under my supervision, she should recover with no complications. Rest is the best cure in these cases."

"When can I travel?" Catherine wanted to know at once.

Dr. Pérez frowned and wagged a finger at her. "That should not concern you for the time being. We must watch that condition carefully before deciding something like that."

"We sent a telegram to your parents," María Lucía put in, "telling them that you had been delayed. We didn't know what else to say, of course, but at least that kept them from going to the airport to meet you."

"Oh, thank you," Catherine sighed. "How clever of you to think of it. Home seems so far away right now. Did they send any message back?" She could imagine that Alex would be beside himself with annoyance.

"No, so far there's been no answer," María Lucía assured her.

"Come along, come along," Violet said suddenly. "We'll let Catherine rest for a while and she can tell us about her adventures later." She stood up and motioned for María Lucía to do the same. After a few more general remarks from Dr. Pérez, the three trooped out. Catherine smiled to herself as she heard Frank and María Lucía talking at the foot of the stairs. Although she could not hear what they said, the conversation lasted for several minutes and she was satisfied that Frank had taken her remarks to heart.

After Frank left, the house became very quiet—probably on orders from Violet—and Catherine tried to sleep. There was too much light in the room, however, and the air was stuffy. She lay on one side, feeling helpless and irritable. Alex, she noted, had not written to her after the first letter, while she had sent

156

him at least a note nearly every day. But of course he would see no reason to write; she had only gone on a short vacation and would soon come back to him. He could put her out of his mind until then. Well, she would just see about that. Men! And there was Frank Gibson. In his bumbling way, probably unconsciously, he had tried to use her to make María Lucía jealous; fortunately she had seen through that nearly from the beginning.

And César . . . she really should be angriest of all with him. Even though he had said nothing definite to her—and indeed it seemed that he had been particularly careful not to say anything concrete, always stopping short of the direct statement—he had led her to hope, to believe, oh, a multitude of things. She wished that she had asked him about Eugenia de las Casas in those last moments as he held her hand, for he had been vulnerable then and he would have told her anything she wanted to know. Perhaps there were others she should have asked about as well. She sighed heavily. What she really wished right then, more than anything, was to flee her pain and problems, to be a child again, sleeping under the slant of the roof in her grandmother's house, with the air as cold and sweet as winter apples.

Although Catherine insisted that she could get up for dinner, the Imberts had a tray sent up to her. Afterward María Lucía came in for a visit. "I don't want to tire you out," she cautioned, "but I just wanted to see how you are. Did you have a good time, except for your accident?"

Catherine obliged her with a full report of her visit. She wanted to know what kind of an impression her story would make on a third party. María Lucía listened carefully, asking a question once in a while. When Catherine had finished, María Lucía threw up her hands. "How can you lie there so calmly? If all that had happened to me, I'm sure I would be a nervous wreck."

"Who says I'm calm?" Catherine retorted. Reliving the past sixty hours had in fact set her heart pounding; she wasn't sure her nerves would ever be the same again.

"I don't know what to make of it," María Lucía said. "The sister sounds as if she might be jealous of you, but then César would have had to give her some reason to be. I wonder what he told her about you."

"So do I," Catherine returned. "Do you know anything about Eugenia de las Casas?" she added in a rush.

María Lucía frowned. "Where did you meet her?"

"I didn't. I think César has been seeing her and I just wondered what kind of person she is."

María Lucía began to pace the room, lacing and unlacing her fingers·as she walked. She seemed unable to keep still; nevertheless, she attended to Catherine's question. "I haven't kept up with people very well. Because I was away at school for so long, I lost interest, I guess. But I suppose Eugenia is what you would call a poor little rich girl. She went to an expensive boarding school in Switzerland, I know, is very well educated in all the social graces, and speaks several languages. She dresses beautifully, doesn't need to work, plays in tennis tournaments. Let's see, what else—"

"Ugh, I don't think I want to hear any more," Catherine blurted out. "Let me ask you about you instead. How are you and Frank getting along?"

Stars danced in María Lucía's eyes. "He was so different this afternoon. I don't understand it," she said in a bewildered tone. "Not at all distant, as he has been. Why, did he say anything to you on the way?"

"We did talk a little," Catherine said evasively, "and

that's why I want to ask you whether it was your parents who forbade you to see Frank or whether it was someone else."

"But of course it was my parents. Who else could it be?" María Lucía asked.

"Eduardo?"

"Why do you say Eduardo?" asked María Lucía.

"I'm not sure exactly, but for one thing, Frank says it was Eduardo who told him not to see you anymore."

María Lucía sat down on the bed and thought hard. When she looked up, her face was troubled. She said slowly, "You are awakening a suspicion which I had long forgotten. Now that you mention it, I don't think my mother said much about Frank at all. In fact, I only remember one conversation with her which concerned him. That was after he had stopped telephoning, though." She screwed her eyes shut and tried to recall the situation. "I can't remember exactly what we said—I've probably repressed it—but I know my mother said that his behavior toward me didn't surprise her, from what she had heard about him."

"But what had she heard?" Catherine pressed, "and from whom?"

"It was so long ago . . . something about selling land up near his farm . . . something Eduardo had told her about." María Lucía's eyes blazed. "Yes! Eduardo! It had something to do with his law firm!"

Catherine tried to concentrate through the pain of her headache. The aspirin she had swallowed an hour before had only taken the edge off. "Could it be possible," she suggested, "that Eduardo has been playing a double game? Could he have made both you and Frank believe that it was your parents who objected, when all the time it was he and no one else?"

"It was Eduardo who told me how angry Mother and Daddy were. He said that I shouldn't even mention the subject to them, that he would try to intercede for me."

"But why didn't you go straight to them?" Catherine wondered. "I thought you were close. You and your mother seem to communicate well."

"I don't know," María Lucía said wretchedly. "It sounded just plausible enough, I suppose. My father does have some old-fashioned ideas and you know how forceful my mother can be—I am no match for her in an argument. Another reason was that I was so hurt—it was the first time they had ever forbade me to do anything. They've always trusted my judgment."

"Don't you think you ought to ask them now? Certainly something strange has been going on," Catherine said wearily. "I'm sorry but I really have to rest now. My head feels funny."

"Oh, that brother of mine. If he's at the bottom of this—" María Lucía shook her clenched fist at the ceiling. "Okay, you try to sleep and I'll tell you what I find out."

The next day Catherine saw little of the Imberts. When the maid brought her meals or came to clean the room, she would ask where they were; and always the Señorita María Lucía was speaking with her mother or was on the telephone with her father. Catherine did not even know whether her friend went to work or not. In the late afternoon María Lucía looked in briefly to see how Catherine was feeling.

"Eduardo is coming here to dinner. Then we'll see what has been going on behind my back," she vowed.

Between dozes Catherine heard Eduardo arrive just after dark. Her supper tray was late, which led her to theorize that the family discussion had begun immediately in the living room and dinner had been held back. After she had finished her meal and the tray had been removed, she selected at random several volumes from the bookcase near her bed. Most of the books in the room were popular novels of the twenties and thirties with Violet's maiden name on the flyleaf in violet ink. She opened one called *The Green Hat* and soon submerged herself in the narrative. But after a while she noticed that she couldn't recall what had happened five pages before, and then, when she turned back to the page immediately preceding the one she was reading, whole paragraphs struck her as completely new. Finally the words turned into black ants that crawled aimlessly around on the page, resisting all efforts to herd them back into comprehensible sentences. The next thing she knew, light streamed into the windows and someone knocked at her door.

"I came to see you last night, but you were already asleep," María Lucía announced briskly as she came to sit in the chair by Catherine's bed. She looked stunning in an orange dress with white piping and accents of chalk-white summer jewelry. Although there were circles under her eyes, her general appearance was relaxed and collected.

"I fell asleep over my reading," Catherine yawned. "How did it go last night?"

María Lucía shook her head. "I still can't believe it. Eduardo constructed the most elaborate ruse and it almost worked—if you hadn't stepped in. He has always been one to hold grudges and he had one against Frank. We couldn't get the whole story out of him last night but my father has ways of finding out. I think it is pretty certain that Eduardo was in the wrong."

"What did he do?"

"It's what he didn't do. We think that he was representing some people who wanted to buy land adjoining Frank's. They wanted a particular tract that wasn't included in the deed and there was some attempt to alter boundaries or alter the deed—as I said, we aren't sure yet. But somehow Frank blocked the attempt."

"I'm sorry that the family is involved," Catherine said. "Of course I never dreamed that it was anything like this when I started asking questions. Your parents must feel terrible."

"Oh, they do and so do I," María Lucía said. "The only good thing about it is that they see Frank in a new light. Eduardo has never tried to do anything unethical before, but his ambitions got the better of him. He wants to be in politics, you see, and he thought that the businessmen who wanted the land would appreciate the favor he tried to do for them and help him in return. When the deal fell through, he was humiliated and wanted revenge. Not long after that, Frank and I started dating and he saw his chance."

"You mean you were his means of vengeance?" Catherine asked.

"Yes. When he saw how much we liked each other, he went to Frank and, supposedly speaking for the entire family, said that he was not to come to the house anymore. In fact, Eduardo hoped that I would meet someone who would be useful to him politically."

"I don't understand why Frank didn't connect the two incidents," Catherine commented.

"I don't think he ever knew that Eduardo was behind the real estate operation," María Lucía surmised.

"And your parents knew nothing either?"

"Nothing," María Lucía stated. "Now, of course, my father is furious with Eduardo and my mother has taken all the blame upon herself. She says that she was too permissive a parent—that she should have meddled more in both our affairs so that she would at least have known what was going on!"

"Now I see why Eduardo insisted on accompanying us to Frank's farm. He was afraid the two of you might figure out what had happened once you had a chance to talk."

"Either that or he wanted to observe us together and see if we already suspected. He didn't make the effort to come to the party I gave for you and only found out afterward that Frank had been invited and that furthermore, we were to visit Frank. I'm sure that made him nervous. But apparently he relaxed enough during the day at the farm so that he didn't mind us staying at the house while you took a walk with him and Clarita. That was probably because Frank was so interested in you."

"You can't say that any longer," Catherine reminded her. "Does Frank know anything about all this?"

"No, but he will soon. My brother will never apologize to him, but I will." María Lucía smiled.

The two friends looked at each other with resignation. "Another crisis weathered," Catherine sighed. "Isn't it awful what some people will do to have their own way? But I don't think Eduardo would have succeeded in keeping you two apart forever. Some people are meant to find each other."

CHAPTER NINE

BUSINESSMEN CONVENE IN ADVISORY SESSION
Cali, January 8 — Yesterday the Hotel Intercontinental was the scene of a banquet that marked the official opening of a three-day series of discussions on the trade balance of Colombia and her place in the world market. . . . Representatives of several foreign governments attended, among which . . . In his remarks welcoming the delegates, the Minister of Agriculture noted . . .

Catherine skimmed the newspaper report as she drank her morning coffee. Her eyes first had been attracted by the picture accompanying the article and its lengthy caption, which read in part, "Don César Saavedra Solano, owner of Los Limonares and San Andrés, greets the Venezuelan Minister of Agriculture at the reception held at his home in Cali. . . ." Catherine carefully folded the newspaper so that only the accompanying article showed and then read it again with more attention. From what she could gather, it appeared that César was one of the local hosts for an international conference on trade, a convention that drew both representatives from foreign countries and prominent Colombians from each sector of the country's economic life. That might explain why she had not heard from him personally since her return from Los Limonares.

She examined the photograph again. She had just gotten used to César as a practical kind of gentleman farmer, one who solved the daily problems of running a hacienda by rolling up his sleeves and getting his hands dirty. But the picture in the newspaper presented another facet of him, one that she had only glimpsed before, that of an executive, at ease in international society, who gave elegant parties at his town house. How little she knew about him, she thought wistfully, so little that even the briefest newspaper caption could tell her something she didn't know. San Andrés must be another plantation, another part of his life she hadn't touched.

In the photograph, which was fairly clear in spite of being overexposed, César flashed his magnetic smile at the rotund, bespectacled gentleman whose hand he was shaking. As he leaned toward the Venezuelan dignitary who commanded his attention, with his other hand he was bringing another gentleman forward to be presented. Even at that remove Catherine felt the charisma, and precisely because of his literal and social distance from her, as represented by the photograph, she experienced again the doubt that was assailing her of late. She knew virtually nothing about his past or his plans for the future. He was probably disgusted by her stupid behavior during the flood. She was too plain. He was too important. The objections were building into a litany of pain.

To shake off her mood Catherine got to her feet and began fussing around the room, opening and shutting drawers, straightening books in the shelves. She must not let the external trappings of wealth and position dazzle her. As two ordinary people, she and César had understood each other.

When she had finished tidying the already tidy dressing table, she paused in the center of the room and surveyed her surroundings. Her two suitcases and her purse waited by the door. Aside from the breakfast tray and a stiff floral arrangement on the windowsill, the room gave no indication that anyone had occupied it recently. She crossed to the flowers, extracted a card from their midst, and slipped it into the pocket of her sky-blue traveling suit. She had read the words on it a hundred times and they said no more on the hundredth reading than they had on the first, although she kept imagining each time she finished reading that there was some message she had missed. The card was identical to the one that had accompanied her lost suitcase when it had arrived at the Imberts' on her first night in Cali. She pictured César scrawling the same formal message with an ironic flourish: With the compliments of César Saavedra Solano. She had expected something more personal, in fact, and much preferred the hastily arranged bowl of camellias that he had sent to her room at Los Limonares.

Since her return to the Imberts', she had had no direct word from him, but only the cold, expensive floral display. His apparent neglect had hurt and annoyed her. But most of all, it had made her anxious: she was afraid that she would have to leave the country without seeing him again.

At the sound of voices downstairs, she took up her purse and started out the door. She was halfway down the stairs when she turned and ran back for the front page of the newspaper, which she folded up and slipped into her purse.

All was chaos in the fern room. Violet Imbert, wearing a suit and turban in a particularly aggressive shade of purple, knelt in a sea of lists and folders, while María Lucía struggled to shut an overnight bag that stood bulging on the table. As Violet jotted notes on a pad in front of her, she barked orders to the cook, who hovered above her. On her way into the room, Catherine was passed by a maid who had been dispatched to find a folder that María Lucía had misplaced.

"Oh, there you are, we were just about to send for you," María Lucía said as she worried the zipper of the bag shut, slipped a small padlock on the end, and came to sit down. "Mother and I are going to share a cab downtown and we have a few minutes to chat before it's time to go."

Violet got to her feet, still clutching her notepad and pen, and took a seat beside her daughter. "I do want to apologize again, Catherine," she said. "We would like to go to the airport with you, of course, but these plans were made before we knew you would be staying this long. Not that we haven't enjoyed every minute," she hastened to add.

"Please don't apologize," Catherine said. "I would feel awful if I disrupted your schedules any more than I already have."

"It's partly my fault for having planned too many things to do this month," Violet said. "This morning, for example, I have a meeting of the committee on the orphanage. I will probably have to leave that early to make the luncheon meeting of the arts council—construction of the new community theater starts next week and there are still a million details to decide on. Ordinarily I would skip my bridge group in the afternoon, but this week we're giving a party for one of our members who is moving to Panama. So you see—" She spread her hands wide.

"I think your visit is ending too soon as it is," María Lucía said. "I can't believe you're going today." She paused as the maid returned with the misplaced folder, which she slipped into an attaché case. "I'm a little bit nervous," she admitted. "I've never led a tour before and this one is overnight. What if I lose a tourist? What if someone gets sick?"

"You'll do beautifully. And you need to know that part of the travel business," Catherine encouraged her. "By the way, you certainly were efficient about getting my ticket changed." Only the day before, the doctor had pronounced Catherine well enough to make the journey home. María Lucía had managed to find a cancellation on the plane leaving the next afternoon. After waiting so many days to be told she could travel, Catherine was not sure that she was ready to leave after all.

"I was just lucky," María Lucía demurred. "Give your parents my love when you get home. What will you tell them was the high point of your trip?"

"Oh my, I don't know," Catherine said, wrinkling her brow. "The bullfights were interesting, and the party for me, and—oh, I guess I should include the flood, shouldn't I?"

"You . . . haven't heard from César Saavedra, have you, dear?" Violet inquired cautiously. "I would be inclined to say that meeting him was one of the high points."

Catherine blushed. She had been aware for days that Violet's curiosity about César would have to be satisfied sooner or later, but she had nothing certain to tell her. "I suppose he's very busy. You saw the article in the paper? I have it right here." She took the newspaper from her purse and spread it out on the low table around which they were seated, pretending all the while not to see the look the two women exchanged over her head.

"Then he doesn't know you're leaving today," María Lucía said finally. "Don't you think you should tell him?"

"I—don't know," Catherine said. "I don't know whether it would be proper or not, although I would like to thank him for his kindness to me. What do you think?" She looked from one to the other.

Violet spoke up first. "All things considered, I think it would be all right. After all, you will be leaving and you won't have another opportunity to thank him. Why not phone him this morning? You have nothing to lose."

Catherine breathed a sigh of relief. She had needed someone to tell her it was all right to do what she was going to do anyway.

María Lucía glanced at her wristwatch. "We're going to have to go soon—I'd better telephone for a cab."

When her daughter had left the room, Violet reached over and patted Catherine's hand. "Let us know all about your plans when you get home—the wedding and all that."

Catherine looked away, then back at Violet. It would be the first time she said it aloud. "There won't be any wedding."

"What?" Violet sat forward. "But surely this is a recent development? Since you arrived here?"

"Yes," Catherine nodded. "I think I probably would have come to the same conclusion had I stayed home. But making the trip put enough distance between me and Alex so that I saw what a mistake our marriage would have been. In fact, I wouldn't be surprised if, subconsciously, the trip wasn't a desperate attempt on my part to find breathing room. To tell you the truth, I think we bore each other and have for years."

"María Lucía told me that Alex was opposed to your visiting us," Violet commented.

"Bitterly opposed."

"He probably knew what would happen," Violet nodded. "Yes, I'll bet dollars to doughnuts that he saw the break coming. But what will you do now?"

"Why, I don't know," Catherine replied vaguely. "Just go on as I have been, I suppose."

"And what about this business with César? That had nothing to do with breaking off your engagement, did it?" Violet inquired too casually. But at the look of pain that swept Catherine's face, she caught her breath. "Oh, my dear," she said in a low voice, "I didn't know."

"The taxi is already here. Of all times for them to be prompt," María Lucía said as she hurried in to gather up her overnight bag and papers. Violet swooped down on the sheets lying about the floor and stuffed them into an enormous handbag. Then they were all hugging each other and crying a little and babbling last-minute instructions and good-byes.

"You'll get to the airport all right?" María Lucía fretted as they walked to the front door together. "I wish Daddy hadn't gone on that business trip. It's awful that no one is going with you! Maybe I can at least give you a call from somewhere during the day."

"Don't worry, I'm a big girl," Catherine said. "I got here, didn't I?"

"I've told the cook you'll be here for lunch," Violet broke in. "That's right, isn't it?"

"I guess so," Catherine said. "Good-bye again, and thank you for everything."

María Lucía and Violet hugged Catherine for the last time and started out the door, but as she passed, Violet caught Catherine by the sleeve and whispered in her ear, "Make that phone call, do you hear me? Don't leave this city until you do."

"I will," Catherine promised, although the prospect of doing so terrified her. She stood on the doorsill waving until the taxi had disappeared around the corner, then went back inside and collapsed in a chair in the living room. Violet was right. She had only a few hours left. Unless she took matters into her own hands, she would never see or hear from César again.

Still she lingered, gathering courage. Would she interrupt some important appointment? If he could not find time to call her, was it not better just to go quietly? Finally she made herself climb the stairs to the telephone in the upper hall, where she was less likely to be disturbed. She had, she reminded herself, nothing to lose. Nothing except everything.

She almost hoped that his Cali number would not be in the telephone book, but it was. The first time she dialed, she got through half of the numbers, then hung up the receiver, her heart pounding. The next time she forced herself to continue and heard the ring at the other end of the line. An impersonal voice told her that she had reached the Saavedra residence. Could she speak to don César? she asked. The voice wanted to know who was calling. After she said her name, there was a long pause and the sound of paper rustling, as if someone were searching through a list. Finally the voice told her that don César was not at home. When would he be at home? Catherine wanted to know. She suspected that he was there at that moment, but that he had instructed a servant to limit his calls. Later, the voice told her, don César would be home at a later time. Catherine thanked the voice and hung up. Desperation gripped her. As she stared blankly, trying to decide what to do, her eyes fell on a scrap of paper beside the telephone. There, in María Lucía's handwriting, lay the names and numbers of two taxicab companies. Catherine picked up the receiver again and dialed the first number before she had time to argue herself out of it.

The tall apartment building stood on the Avenida Colombia, overlooking the river. After she had paid the driver, Catherine hesitated a moment, scanning the front of the building and half-expecting to see a familiar silhouette in one of the windows. But the facade yielded nothing except a toy poodle running back and forth on one of the upper balconies.

The uniformed doorman informed her that don César Saavedra occupied the eleventh floor. In the elevator Catherine tried to formulate a few phrases, something to get her through the first uncertain moments, but her mind was a blank. Then it occurred to her that he might have guests or might actually be holding a meeting there, and she began to regret her rashness. Had the elevator opened onto a public hall, she might have merely waited for it to return and have gone back to the Imberts' without trying to see him. But while she argued with herself, the elevator operator opened the door and announced the eleventh floor. When Catherine alighted, she found herself in a foyer that was obviously part of César's apartment and she realized that he must indeed inhabit the entire level. The elevator door had closed behind her. She felt vulnerable, as if she were being secretly watched. The only thing to do was to knock on the forbidding door in front of her.

It was opened by a smartly uniformed young woman who bore little outward resemblance to the more casual, even motherly, servants of Los Limonares. When the woman spoke, Catherine recognized the officious voice of the telephone. No, don César was not at home, she replied again. However, since he was expected at any time, Catherine could wait if she liked with the other lady.

"If you could just tell him that Catherine Gray was here. I was just . . . passing by," Catherine said, without knowing why. She really would have preferred to leave no message.

The servant agreed to relay the message and started to close the door.

"No, just a moment. I think I will wait after all," Catherine decided. If others were waiting to see César, she could too. She had come too far to turn around.

Catherine allowed herself to be ushered into an L-shaped living room carpeted and furnished in off-white. The young woman who lolled on the oyster-colored sofa might have dressed that morning with César's living room in mind, for her ruby-red dress made her the focal point of the entire room. She looked Catherine up and down brazenly as the latter approached, then calmly extinguished her cigarette in an onyx ashtray that rested on a beaten-brass table in front of the sofa. For a split second Catherine imagined that she had been recognized but dismissed it as an impossibility. Since the girl did not appear inclined to speak first, Catherine said uncertainly, "Good morning. I hope I'm not intruding, I only—"

"Oh, but you have."

"I beg your pardon?" Catherine racked her brain to remember where she had seen the young woman before. She had expected to see someone with a businesslike manner waiting for an appointment, not a girl lounging about as if she were in her own home.

"You have intruded, haven't you? And I don't believe you told me your name." The young woman looked smugly at Catherine from behind a thick fringe of false eyelashes. She had removed her shoes and sat swinging one leg carelessly against the sofa, the other leg tucked under her. She seemed dangerously comfortable and accustomed to her surroundings.

Later Catherine berated herself for having been so easily cowed. But at the time, aware only of her intrusion, she stammered, "My name is Catherine Gray. I believe I will be going now."

"The little schoolteacher! Of course!" The girl sat up and clapped her hands gleefully, but there was no humor in her smile, which was as thin and sour as a slice of lemon. Again Catherine had the impression that her identity came as no surprise.

"I'm afraid you have the advantage of me," Catherine said, to remind the girl of her manners. Expecting no civil answer, however, she did not wait for one. "If you will excuse me," she said, and turned to go.

"I am Eugenia de las Casas."

Catherine froze. Of course. Suddenly she recognized the flawless skin and great almond eyes, although from up close Eugenia's features were somewhat coarser than she had imagined them. She merely nodded at the name and remarked, "Pleased to meet you. But I must be going."

"Just a minute." Eugenia's voice had a cutting edge now. "Be sure that you do go and keep going. 'Fools rush in where angels fear to tread,' Miss Gray."

"I'm afraid I don't know what you're talking about," Catherine said coldly, but the sinking feeling in the pit of her stomach told her that she did.

Eugenia de las Casas swung her feet to the floor and leaned slowly forward, like a snake uncoiling. "We are going to be coy, are we?" she hissed. "All right then, I'll tell you what I'm talking about. César Saavedra."

The name hung in the air like a pistol shot. Catherine sank into a chair seconds before her knees would have buckled. "He has been very kind to me. I only

174

came to thank him," she murmured. Terrified, she looked up. A mask of cold fury looked back at her.

"César usually picks cleverer ones," Eugenia sneered. "Don't you think I can see through that little ruse? He has thrown you over and you can't believe it, so you've come to beg for an audience with him. You should have saved yourself the trouble. If he paid you any attention at all, it was only because he wanted a little entertainment, a change of pace for an afternoon or two."

"That is insulting to him and to me," Catherine spat out, her timidity swallowed by a rising tide of anger.

Eugenia drummed her long, scarlet nails irritably on the arm of the sofa. "You," she said, "what do you know about César?"

"I know enough to know that he is not what you imply he is," Catherine answered staunchly. Nevertheless the challenge struck home. What did she know of him, indeed?

Eugenia laughed an ugly, flat laugh and shook her head in mock pity. "How little you've seen of him. I understand César because he is like me. We take what we want and we don't make mistakes. We are shrewd and strong and we will endure together long after you have left this country, which I suggest you do immediately."

"I am not accustomed to being told what to do, especially by total strangers," Catherine said levelly. Her head was beginning to throb from tension and her palms were sweating. "And furthermore, it seems to me that someone as shrewd and strong as César can handle his own affairs without anyone's help."

"César is also a busy man. He doesn't have time to be bothered by little provincials on their first trip abroad. Did you think he was included in the price of your ticket? He isn't a tourist attraction. He will be grateful that I saved him the trouble of getting rid of you."

Apparently Eugenia considered her remarks conclusive, for she turned haughtily away to light another cigarette. Then she threw back her head, blew smoke at the ceiling, and closed her eyes, as if she were relaxing alone.

But Catherine was not yet vanquished. She had been caught unawares by Eugenia's presence. It was only too clear that Eugenia had the run of César's apartment, a fact that suggested a certain degree of intimacy between the two. Nevertheless, Catherine was proud; and if she was to be defeated in her hopes, still she refused to give Eugenia the satisfaction of knowing it. She had learned something from the problems of Frank and María Lucía, too, and she surmised that she must be a real threat to Eugenia's claims in order for the girl to behave with such unconscionable rudeness.

"I can't help wondering about some things," Catherine said. "In the first place, I'm wondering how you know so much about me and why you bothered to find out. In the second place, I'm wondering what your relationship to César really is. You talk as if you owned him. And yet if you did, you would not have to say these monstrous things to me."

A dull flush spread over Eugenia's high cheekbones. "Anyone who is not a fool or a stranger—or both—knows what my relationship to César is. Our families have owned adjoining lands for centuries. They are linked by a wealth of common tastes and traditions. You could never begin to understand it, with your short and uncomplicated pedigree."

"I'm surprised, then, that a person of your breeding would stoop to a discussion like this one," Catherine interposed, speaking a little louder than necessary to keep her voice from trembling.

176

Eugenia's eyes narrowed. "I do as I please. I'm impulsive, madcap, a little mad, even. And I always get my way."

For a fleeting moment at the beginning, Catherine had had the wild hope that she could turn the tide of the argument. But deep inside she knew that all she had was words. Even if she won, the verbal battle with Eugenia had nothing to do with the circumstances. Eugenia was rude and perhaps unprincipled, but her position was strong. Catherine was an outsider in César's life and she, obviously, was not.

All of a sudden it seemed pointless to continue and the realization made her weary. With an effort that she tried to hide, she stood up. "Miss De las Casas, you seem to think it was I who pursued and ensnared César. Believe me when I say that I have never made a move that was not in response to an initiative taken by him. Besides"—she hesitated as despair suddenly welled up inside her—"I'm sure you have overestimated his interest in me. So if you will excuse me, at last, I think there is nothing more to say."

Eugenia rose also. She had sensed Catherine's momentary weakness and could almost taste victory. "If you really care about him," she said in a voice that was suddenly honeyed, sympathetic, "you will want what is best for him. That is what I want, after all. So of course you must give him up, mustn't you?" She inclined her head sadly, as if she regretted the truth of her words. "You don't belong here and you would never belong. César deserves an equal. Only that would make him happy."

"I don't need your pity," Catherine said through clenched teeth. She was disgusted with herself and with the whole situation. "Evidently you think you are his equal. But you don't mind casting aspersions on his character in order to get him. I don't believe he is like

177

you because I don't believe that he is heartless and cruel." She turned on her heels.

"So you are going to play the righteous martyr, are you?" Eugenia shrilled. "Then let me tell you something I'm sure César didn't mention, something that will help along your martyrdom. He already has a wife."

Catherine threw over her shoulder in disgust, "You're bluffing. César wouldn't have—" She stopped at the sound of feet hurrying after her.

"Come back here!" Eugenia caught Catherine's hand and pulled her back into the living room. Catherine was so appalled that she couldn't protest. Leaving Catherine in the center of the room, Eugenia strode to the sofa, where she had left her purse. She clawed furiously through the contents until at last she held up what appeared to be a small Testament bound in dark green leather. She shook it at Catherine. "I swear to you," she said dramatically, "that César Saavedra was married eight years ago. I know because I attended the wedding."

For several moments Catherine stood arrested in an attitude of departure, like Daphne when, in midflight, she felt herself turning into the laurel tree. Then, getting a hold on her emotions, she turned without a word and walked to the door.

"You wouldn't have him now, would you? But I would. And I will!" Eugenia called after her. Just then the telephone rang on the table between them and Eugenia boldly answered it. As Catherine went out she heard her say, "Oh, hello, darling. I dropped by to let you take me to lunch, but the maid says you have more horrible meetings this afternoon—"

Somehow Catherine found a taxi and made her way back to the Imbert home. After stopping by the kitchen to tell the cook that she did not want any lunch, she went straight to her room and lay face down on the bed. She lay there for an indeterminate time, during which her body and mind were paralyzed with shock. The telephone call had been the last straw; she was sure Eugenia had been talking to César. Never had Catherine's status as an intruder been more clear to her than at that moment when César's voice had reached into the room she was in, to speak to another woman. She did not try to make all the pieces of the puzzle that was César fit together and she did not question Eugenia's information, because she remembered some incidents that seemed to support the horrible contention. She recalled the indistinct form of the hatted girl who appeared in the photographs in Isabel's room. In both pictures she had been standing by César. Again she heard the maid Arcelia nervously breaking off after saying, "Don César has not given a serenade since—" Who else could be lurking in the shadows of Los Limonares but she, the unmentioned wife? More than once, Catherine remembered, she had had the impression that César had stopped short of telling her something of special significance. Then she recalled that he had never mentioned the other property, San Andrés, to her either; his wife must be there. Humiliation began to spread over her, as a drop of ink bleeds across a fresh blotter, and she started to cry softly. At first she cried out of shame and then out of rage. Great, racking sobs shook her and she wept aloud as she had not done since she was a child. Finally, her initial reactions spent, she cried for the deepest reason, the only reason: César. Whatever he had done to her and for whatever reason, César was gone.

In the street an itinerant cobbler shouted out his willingness and proven ability to repair any shoe. Catherine sat up and wiped the back of her hand across her eyes. Hearing the street sounds brought back the first morning of her visit and how full of innocent promise the world had seemed then. It was too early by far to go to the airport, but she wanted to leave immediately. As soon as she arrived there, she told herself, her trip would be effectively finished. Fortunately, since her movements no longer depended upon anyone in the world, she could leave whenever she wished. She longed to be gone, to start her own new year.

Catherine straightened her clothing and sat down at the dressing table to do something about her face. In the corner of the mirror still stuck the postcard view of the valley, which César had given her. It mocked her cruelly, like a letter that arrives after its sender has died, and started her tears afresh. She took it down and, together with the card in her pocket and the newspaper article about the trade conference, threw it in the wastebasket. Then she went into the bathroom, wrung out a washcloth in cold water, and held it over her eyes until the cloth became tepid. That removed the red blotches from her face, but the skin around her eyes was still swollen smooth as cream. On her way back to her room she telephoned for a taxi. After a final check of the closet and drawers, she carried her suitcases downstairs without calling the maid and went outside to wait on the sidewalk for the cab. Within ten minutes she was giving instructions to the driver and was looking forward to relaxing for the first time that day. But just as the driver was pulling away from the curb, another taxi appeared from the opposite direction, making for the Imbert home.

"Yoo-hoo, Catherine!" Violet was leaning out the window, waving. The two taxis came to a halt beside each other a few yards from the door. "The arts council is waiting for me—I left the budget somewhere in the house! Good heavens, you're not going to the airport already?"

"Yes, it's best to be early for international flights," Catherine said, knowing it was an inadequate excuse.

Violet leaned farther out the window so that she could get a better look at Catherine. "Why, you've been crying!" she shouted. "Whatever is the matter?"

"Nothing," Catherine lied, fervently thankful that the people in the neighboring houses probably did not understand English.

"Did you call that Saavedra man?" Violet demanded.

"Yes . . . no," Catherine hemmed.

"What's that?" Violet shouted.

"I mean, I went to see him but he wasn't there," Catherine said.

"You tried to see him?" Violet asked with such interest that Catherine could have kicked herself for mentioning it. "But what happened? You look absolutely stricken."

"Nothing. Good-bye," Catherine called.

"You could write him a letter when you get home," Violet shouted.

Catherine shook her head. "I don't think so."

The door of the Imbert house opened and a maid, doubtless informed of their presence by Violet's shouting, came out onto the walk. *"El teléfono, señora, muy importante,"* she announced.

"Oh, bother, the telephone," Violet spluttered. "Can't you wait even a minute, dear?"

"I'll write you a letter—it's nothing that can be helped," Catherine volunteered. "I'd rather go on now. Good-bye, and thanks again for everything."

As her taxi sped away, Catherine closed her eyes and let her head fall back against the seat. She had broken out in a cold sweat and was limp with relief at having escaped Violet's questioning. María Lucía and her mother would soon forget about César Saavedra. After all, he had only loomed large in Catherine's imagination and would have been an even more illusory presence to the Imberts. By the time they thought, someday, to inquire about him in a letter, the story would be ancient history. Maybe she could even escape telling them altogether. Ahead still lay the confrontation with Alex and the subsequent minor confrontations with alarmed family members and friends. There was no way of explaining her decision so that any of them would understand. If she mentioned César, Alex would tell her that she had merely been infatuated with him and that infatuation is an ephemeral state, impossible to sustain. In her heart she knew it was not infatuation; but whatever it was, it didn't matter anymore. After she had broken the engagement, she would be free and independent. She did not really want to be free and independent, if that meant refusing to form lasting bonds with another human being. But above all she meant to preserve her integrity. She could not do so by marrying a man she did not love, or by entering into a liaison with one she did.

Alex would miss her for a little while, the way one misses a piece of furniture one has grown accustomed to seeing in a particular spot; but when a useful table or chair gets broken, one buys another to take its place. Before long, with daily use of the new one, the individuality of the old one is forgotten. As for César, she probably had not made a strong enough impression on him even to be missed.

Catherine sighed. Once more the road before her was straight and clear. She would keep on teaching school. She would save her money, but perhaps spend some for travel, for in spite of the unsettling aspects of her trip to Colombia, she found that she loved the thrill of new places. She need never worry again about making the mistakes she had made on her first journey. Perhaps Greece one spring and a week sometime in London, going to the theater. . . . Automatically in her imagination she heard César's voice teasing her. *What? So young and already behaving as if your life is over? There are other fish in the sea, my dear, and you'll soon be spreading your net again!* She found herself shaking her head in emphatic denial, as if he were there to see her.

The trip to the airport was interminable. When she had driven over the same road with César, it had seemed a reasonable length and spiced with interesting sights. She sat motionless, looking neither to the right nor left, intent on her destination. She had been running on nervous energy all day and it was beginning to drain away.

Although her self-esteem was at its nadir, she could at least congratulate herself on having helped María Lucía. The discovery of Eduardo's guile had caused the Imberts to reassess themselves as a family. Violet concluded that, had they been as close-knit a family as they thought they were, Eduardo would neither have felt the need nor had the opportunity to insinuate himself between his parents and his sister for his own purposes. After Eduardo got over his anger at being exposed and was ready to listen to reason, his parents hoped to take a more active role in helping him plan his career. Catherine judged that María Lucía and Frank would need no help in coming to their own understanding. But a depressing thought struck her. She, who had always been so careful not to offend, had made two enemies: Eduardo Imbert and Eugenia de las Casas, whose fury still clung around her like the smell of brimstone.

She looked back. The city had disappeared. It was as if she had never been there.

CHAPTER TEN

After Catherine had had her ticket validated and her suitcases checked, she walked restlessly around the long, open-air waiting room, unable to let herself relax until she was on the airplane. Finally, since it was two hours before she had to be cleared through customs, she decided to take the escalator to the restaurant on the U-shaped mezzanine above. Although she was not hungry, she was sure that her tenacious headache was partly due to lack of food.

By the time she had finished a sandwich and a cup of coffee in the half-empty restaurant, she had begun to feel steadier and was able to turn her thoughts to a pleasant reunion with her parents. Finding that she still had an ample supply of Colombian currency, she decided to spend it on presents for them and other family members in the airport gift shops. To that end she passed a methodical quarter of an hour selecting handmade Indian dolls for three little cousins whom she expected to see at Eastertime. From a colorful display of straw and jute handicrafts, she selected some orange-and-yellow placemats for her aunt, a red macramé purse for a fellow teacher, and some coasters to use when the Book Lovers' Circle met at her house. The day she had toured Cali with César, she had bought a few small gifts, and during her afternoon of shopping with Violet she had purchased a faïence bowl for her mother. Now she was drawn to a pair of earrings resting on velvet behind the jewelry counter. They were in the form of cattleyas with petals of filigreed silver and an unpolished emerald in each center. They were as unlike her mother's plain tastes as anything Catherine had ever seen, which was just why she had to buy them. Everyone, her mother included, she thought, deserved a sip of moonlight, a scrap of whimsy, once in a while. "If I had my life to live over," she had once heard a very old woman say, "I'd eat less beans and more ice cream. I'd be brave enough to make more mistakes." Catherine felt a catch in her throat. She, at least, had dared for a moment or two to make mistakes. And she had made them. Why, oh why, did everything have to remind her of César?

Her purchases completed, Catherine strolled back to the other end of the mezzanine and outside onto the observation deck, which ran the length of the western wing of the airport. A plane had just taxied to a stop below the far end and its passengers were beginning to emerge. From the deck families waved and called down excitedly. Catherine remembered a similar scene when she had arrived. She had looked up then, past the trailing flowered vines that spilled from planters along the edge of the observation deck, and had mildly regretted that there had been no one waiting to greet her. At that time it had been because her plane had been delayed and the Imberts hadn't known when to meet her. Now, due to other, equally unforseeable circumstances, she was leaving the same way she had arrived, alone and unnoticed. Through the windows of the restaurant she saw a clock. One hour and she would be on her way home.

A strong breeze barreled down the deck. Catherine sat down on a bench, closed her eyes, and let the breeze cool her cheeks, which still burned from her tears. But her mind was still in a turmoil, with half-formed thoughts chasing each other in circles, so after a while she again began to walk restlessly. She paced to the end of the deck and back, then started over. For the time being, no passenger planes were arriving or departing, so she had the entire area to herself. In the distant sky two Piper Cubs gamboled like frisky lambs. She had gone nearly two-thirds of the way to the end of the promenade when she heard sharp running steps approaching. Keenly aware that she was alone, she grasped her purse and the bags of souvenirs tighter, but did not risk turning around.

In another moment strong arms had spun her around and enfolded her.

"Thank God, I'm not too late," César said as he pressed her to him.

Catherine stared up at him, dumbfounded. For the first time since she had met him, she saw that he was not master of the situation. "Too late for what?" she said icily, breaking his embrace and stooping to retrieve her packages, which lay scattered about them. "If you will excuse me, it is only a short while until my plane leaves and I haven't been cleared through customs yet."

As she started to walk past him, César caught her wrist roughly. "Why are you doing this?" he demanded. "Did you actually intend to leave without telling me?"

When his fingers closed about her wrist, all of the pain inside Catherine curdled into a red rage. "Since when do I have to answer to you?" she shouted. "You think you can live like a feudal lord and run the world according to your own rules. Well, I'm not one of your vassals and I won't let you treat me as if I were. Get out of my way!"

"Oh, no." He was in control again, except for a muscle twitching in his jaw. "You can fight me if you want to, but you're not getting away until we've had this out. I've spent too much time catching up with you." With that he forced her to sit down beside him on a nearby bench.

"I am going home on the next plane and I have absolutely nothing more to say to you," Catherine said, seething.

"If you had left, you would only have inconvenienced me, you know. I would have found you again," César told her.

"Why are you torturing me like this?" Catherine burst out. "Can't you leave me alone? You've had your fun—if it was fun—and now you can go back to your other amusements, which I'm sure are quite sufficient to keep you occupied."

"Such as Eugenia, for example?" he inquired mildly. "Now just be quiet for a while and let me tell you what I have been doing for the past few days. It might interest you in the end."

"In five minutes I am going to stand up and walk downstairs to go through customs. If you don't let me go, I will start screaming."

"I believe you would. I really believe you would," he said with a touch of admiration. "Do you know," he went on, looking down at the toe of his dress boot, "in the event that there is ever an opportunity for you to do so, there is a favor I would like you to do for me."

"A favor?" Catherine frowned, knowing he was trying to distract her.

"Yes, there is someone to whom I would like to be

introduced. A Señora Violet Imbert—is that the person you were visiting? I owe her a debt of gratitude."

"Actually I was visiting her daughter," Catherine said, "but I don't see the relevance—"

A loudspeaker crackled and a muffled voice announced that the passengers for Flight 507 should proceed to the customs area. "I'm afraid I can't give you five minutes after all," Catherine said with finality.

"Yes, you will. You are not getting on that plane." She had half-risen, but the passionate insistence in his voice made her sink down again. "You will listen to everything I have to say," he commanded, "and then, if you still want to go, I will see that you have a first-class seat on the next plane. I give you my word."

A strange paralysis of the will, which she had experienced before in César's presence, stole over Catherine. Again she started to stand, then sat down. Dumbly she nodded her assent, even while she cautioned herself that she must be unyielding, strong.

"That's better," César said. "Listen carefully. This may take some time. We will go back to your last day at Los Limonares. After you left with that fellow—Johnson, whatever his name was—"

"Gibson, Frank Gibson," Catherine interrupted. "I've been wanting to tell you—"

César held up his hand to silence her. Cocking an eyebrow at her with a trace of his former sardonic manner, he promised, "You will get your chance to do some explaining after I have finished. There are questions I may want answered too. But to go back. After you left with Frank Gibson, I was uneasy. I will even admit to you that I could not sleep for several nights. To be sure, the flood had created many problems at Los Limonares and in addition there were arrangements to be made for the trade conference, which even at this moment is proceeding without me. Isabel finally noticed that I was not myself and asked me what was wrong. I told her that something was missing. It had, of course, been missing from my life for some time, but unless one is made aware of the lack, of the emptiness, one lives quite comfortably. But I could no longer do that. I told Isabel so and she agreed with me."

Catherine, listening intently with her head bowed, felt his glance on her then but did not raise her head.

He resumed, "And still I hesitated, making up my mind. I do not know whether it mattered to you or not that I did not call you or try to see you, but it mattered to me. Finally, this morning, I came to a decision. I telephoned you at the Imberts' to ask you to have lunch with me and listen to a story. Yes," he nodded as Catherine looked up quickly, "I called but the maid said you had taken a taxi to the Avenida Colombia. In a moment I will tell you what happened next. But first, here is the story I felt you should hear." He paused, visibly bracing himself.

"When I was growing up, our family divided its time between Los Limonares, which grows sugar cane, and a coffee plantation called San Andrés in the highlands. The land of San Andrés adjoined that of two other families in particular, and the three had much in common, at least since the civil wars, when men from all of them fought together under Colonel Aureliano Buendía. It was natural to assume that in time the families would come to be linked by blood as well as by land and friendship, and in fact it was the specific wish of the members of my parents' generation. Do you understand why I am telling you all this?"

"I'm afraid to guess," Catherine said faintly.

Well-wishers for the passengers on Catherine's flight were beginning to trickle upstairs and station themselves along the railings. César waited until a group had passed the bench before going on. "As I may have told you, I was sent away to be educated. After taking my degrees, I worked in the family exporting business in Bogotá for a time, so that for years I was at home only for short periods—the major holidays and family celebrations. There were, however, these close ties between the three families which seemed to have remained unchanged over the years. When it came time for me to marry—and sometimes those things are decided in cold blood, with little regard for the feelings—my family hoped that I would marry the eldest daughter of our nearest neighbors at San Andrés. We had, in childhood and even early adolescence, adored each other, but we had not spent any time with each other for years. The family connection, however, deceived me, at least, and made me think that we were better acquainted and more suited than we were. When I found out that the engaging child with whom I had grown up no longer existed, it was too late. Even after all these years, it is hard for me to recall a happy moment."

"Eight years," murmured Catherine.

"Yes, eight years ago," he agreed, then turned to her in astonishment. "But how did you know that?"

"I'll tell you when it's my turn to explain," Catherine said. She had been listening almost with indifference, suspending judgment, as if César's story concerned a distant historical incident. Nevertheless, his forthright manner impressed her and she knew he would tell the whole truth, no matter what it entailed.

Though obviously disconcerted by Catherine's interjection, César went on, "You are probably thinking that this is a typical story of two people who married without forethought and had to live with the consequences. I only wish it had been that simple; though if it had been, I would not be sitting here with you. I am not a man who gives up on commitments. But shortly after we were married, Dolores—that was her name—

began to act strangely. She had been high-spirited, given to pranks and tantrums, as a child. As a woman she was subject to wild and unpredictable changes of mood. Her gaiety was as impetuous and ultimately uncontrollable as her discontent, which vented itself in murderous rages. She had a peculiar penchant for breaking mirrors, and if you go to San Andrés today you will not find a single one. Toward the end we had to keep a close watch on all the knives and scissors. But she was cunning and often managed to circumvent our controls. One day, to announce that she had been able to find a pair of scissors, she cut all of the linens—every sheet and towel—neatly in two. After she attacked one of the servants with a pair of scissors because the girl had done a clumsy job of mending a blouse, I placed her under a doctor's care. Then began a series of treatments. At first we were all hopeful that she would recover and lead a normal life. Sometimes she would appear to be better, but never for long. Finally I was told that she should be institutionalized. A very nice private sanatorium was found and I left her there one Sunday morning, expecting to visit her the next week."

"And you knew nothing of this before you were married?" Catherine could not keep from asking.

"I knew nothing, but of course her family knew everything," César said bitterly. "They had deliberately hidden her condition so that through her marriage they might gain at least partial control of San Andrés and Los Limonares. That is the dark side of these wonderful old family ties you have been hearing about. Dolores and I lived at San Andrés all the time then. She had never interested herself in running the household, preferring to stay in her bedroom or visit friends, so her absence was scarcely noticed. But she did not intend to stay at the sanatorium and managed to call an old friend, a girl who was spending the summer nearby. I do not blame the girl for not informing me or her family. Dolores could be incredibly charming when she wanted something. The first we heard of her escape was when the sanatorium director called to report her disappearance. When we learned that the friend and her car were also missing, we could guess what had happened, but we never learned what they intended to do. Several weeks later the car was found at the bottom of a steep hill by a peasant hunting a stray cow. They had missed a sharp curve and the car had caught fire on impact, probably killing them instantly. It is a bizarre story but there are newspaper reports which corroborate part of it. Isabel can verify the rest, if you want."

Remembering the treacherous highway to Frank's farm, Catherine could see how easily such an accident might occur. She put her hand on César's arm. "I'm sorry. Oh, César, I'm so sorry for you and for her."

Abstractedly he covered her hand with his own. In the slanting afternoon light, his face held an infinity of sadness. "For Dolores I am convinced it was a release. And for me as well, although under the circumstances it sounds selfish to say it. But I don't think anyone could have made Dolores well and happy. For one year we were married but I never felt I had a wife. It was a hard way to learn a lesson but I learned it well: Never marry except for love."

"It is frightening," Catherine said soberly as she thought of Alex, "that you can know a person your whole life and then discover that you don't know him at all. I know it can happen because it has happened to me."

"Or you can know someone for only a few days and feel as if you had known her a whole lifetime. It is always a jump in the dark, this business of marriage.

One can only trust one's feelings and hope for the best."

Catherine felt a pleasurable panic rising. "Tell me," she said hastily, "what you did after you couldn't reach me at the Imberts." When he had begun talking, she had been unwilling to hear him out. But she was being drawn along by his voice and had become hungry for every detail.

César leaned back on the bench and draped his arms along its top. "Now we have more time," he said, nodding at the sky. "There goes your plane."

"Oh!" In spite of herself, Catherine started at the sight of the silver wings careening into the distance. With that, she realized the full magnitude of her decision to stay.

César was saying, "When I heard that you had gone to the Avenida Colombia, I guessed that you might have gone to my apartment, though I could not imagine why." He paused, waiting for an explanation.

"To tell you good-bye because I couldn't reach you by phone," Catherine filled in.

"So you did intend to tell me you were leaving."

"At that point, yes. Later I changed my mind."

"Ah. I thought so. You know, you have made a lot of trouble for me. I have been chasing you all day. When I telephoned my apartment to see if you were there, I was astonished to find myself speaking with Eugenia de las Casas."

"Why astonished?" Catherine asked quickly.

César shrugged. "Because I did not expect her to answer my telephone. To my knowledge she has never been in that apartment before in her life."

"But I don't understand. She certainly seemed at home," Catherine insisted.

"She must have put on quite a performance. I sup-

194

pose she was the one who told you I was married eight years ago."

"Yes, she swore on her own Bible that you were married and that she attended the wedding. But she didn't mention that you were a widower," Catherine admitted.

"Her own Bible? I didn't know she carried one with her," César remarked. "That doesn't sound like Eugenia."

"Well, she did today," Catherine informed him. "She had a little green leather Testament in her purse."

César began to laugh. "What a devil! Do you know what she took her oath on? An address book! I have seen her refer to it more than once and I'm sure that is what it was. But what else did she say to you? If I had known that you were leaving this afternoon, I would not have taken the time to bother with Eugenia. When I spoke with her on the phone, she only said that you had been there but that she had made sure you wouldn't be coming back. Since she refused to tell me anything else, I told her to stay at the apartment until I could get there."

"I'm sorry, but I don't understand any of this," Catherine put in.

César had turned to face her. "But don't you see? Eugenia is nothing to me and never has been. This is a day of surprises for everyone. I was surprised by Eugenia's assumption that she had some claim on me. You no doubt were surprised and hurt—I saw it in your eyes—by whatever she said to you. And believe me, Eugenia was surprised to learn that I was not at all pleased by her sending you on your way. Quite the contrary. I was furious that she had interfered."

"But I saw you at the bullring with her. And María Lucía's brother, Eduardo, said that you two were an item in the society columns," Catherine objected.

"That is exactly where we were likely to be seen," César returned calmly. "I generally see Eugenia on big social occasions—at the bullfights, where I often sit with her father, big parties, and so on. Eugenia is a cousin of the other family which has land near San Andrés. She knew Dolores and has not been above trading on that friendship to speak with me. But I had no idea that her interest went so far. As for the gossip columns, well, they are just that—gossip. I remember one occasion, for example, when Eugenia was one of the organizers of a charity ball and asked me to be her escort. We were, of course, photographed leading a waltz and the picture was printed with a caption that hinted that this was really a piece of news.

"At any rate, I think that you don't need to worry about her anymore. Although she would not tell me what she said to you—probably out of embarrassment—she did give me an idea of why she went to the apartment. Early this morning she stopped by Los Limonares with her father, whose ranch is a little to the north of us. I had been thinking of buying some cattle from him and he wanted to discuss it with me. Since I wasn't there, they chatted with Isabel for a while, and she let slip a piece of news which you should have received before anyone. As I said, I had discussed certain matters with Isabel and, like a woman, she knew the course I would follow before I did. Eugenia decided to interfere. I must say, she was overconfident of her ability to influence me. So she came to the apartment to see me. When you walked in, she saw an easier way to accomplish her aim and leaped at it. It showed quick thinking, I give her that. What did she say to you?"

Catherine said, "I don't want to remember. She seemed to know me at once, by the way, even before I'd said my name."

196

"Isabel might have described you," César speculated. "She has an eye for detail and enjoys exercising it. Poor girl, she will be angry when she learns that she was Eugenia's unwitting accomplice."

Catherine said, "Aside from telling me that you were married and that I was socially unacceptable in your milieu"—here César clenched and unclenched his fist—"I believe she said, let's see, that both of you were shrewd and strong and take what you want."

"Eugenia will have to speak for herself," César grinned, "but I'll admit it's a pretty good description of me. But then I already told you that I take—am used to getting—what I want, didn't I?"

"The night of the flood," Catherine replied. "And then I asked you if you knew what you wanted."

"For the first time in years," he said. "But you must put Eugenia out of your mind. I told her that she had presumed a great deal in the first place by coming to see me on such a mission, and that furthermore, her behavior was inexcusable. My only regret is that she hurt you. For that I can never forgive her."

"Yes, it hurt. You don't know how much," Catherine admitted, lowering her head.

"But will you forgive me, Catherine? If I had been more attentive to you, it would never have happened. You would not have had to search for me, nor would Eugenia have learned before you of what I wanted to tell you. More than once I thought of telling you more about myself, but I was afraid you would turn your back on me. I am sorry now that I didn't take the chance."

Catherine wanted to throw her arms around him and tell him none of it mattered anymore, but she couldn't. Instead she only gave an embarrassed nod of understanding.

César seemed to be aware of her heightened emotions, but was holding himself back from them, delaying acknowledgment of them. He continued, "You see how thorough I am being about this confession. After I had seen Eugenia out the door, much in the same spirit with which she banished you, I imagine, I telephoned the Imberts once again and found myself speaking with the Señora Imbert. What a lecture she gave me about trifling with the affections of one Catherine Gray!"

"She didn't!" Catherine was mortified.

"Oh, yes, she did," César chuckled, "and I am grateful to her for it. I would have come to the airport anyway, but after talking with that opinionated woman, I knew that I would follow you even farther if necessary." Gently he took both of Catherine's hands and pulled her around to face him. Catherine scarcely dared to breathe. "Little Colt, why did you try to bolt and run again? Why did you condemn me without a trial, on the basis of hearsay?"

"But some of what Eugenia said was true," Catherine said weakly. "I don't belong in your world."

"No, no, you don't belong on a big farm in the country, where you can ride horses and see things grow and let the wind blow through your hair," he chided her. "That is ninety percent of my world. But you wouldn't know anything about a farm."

"That's not what I mean," Catherine protested. "I mean—"

"No, you belong in your neat little schoolroom, with the desks in perfect rows and a vase of fresh flowers on your desk. What an orderly little life—I'll bet you would never forget to change the water in the vase."

"Teaching is one thing I'm good at," Catherine said defensively.

"One thing among many, I'm sure," he shot back. "But wait a minute. Perhaps I can appeal to your professional interests. Do you remember the little stone chapel at Los Limonares?"

"Yes, it is in front of the house."

"Long ago it used to be a school for the workers' families—ours and others in the area. I was thinking just the other day that it would be good to start the school again. Would you like the job?"

Catherine strained to see his face in the failing light. His customary sangfroid seemed a little too deliberately maintained. "Possibly," she answered, falling in with his game, "only I would have to hear the specific terms of the offer first."

"Of course," he returned gravely. "You did well to ask, because the post carries certain conditions. The reason I hesitated for a week before offering you the position was not because I was unsure of you. Not in the least. It was relatively easy for me to see that you were just the person for it. But I thought you might reject the terms. You would live at Los Limonares and it is not such a glamorous life there. The owner is not a boy anymore, you know, and he must work long hours. He doesn't have as much time to play as a boy would. That is why you should have something to do which you enjoy, such as teaching school. And this owner is a man with certain obligations. He is responsible, for instance, for his sister—"

"Do you think she would like to help with the school?" Catherine asked. Her voice sounded tight and strange and she was abashed at the way hope showed naked in it.

"That might be just the thing for her," César said, and Catherine could tell that he was pleased at her suggestion. Without explaining, he reached across her to pick up her packages. Then he took her arm and began walking her toward the bank of escalators. It was almost dark. In the still evening air Catherine could smell the blended odor peculiar to him, made up of the lingering aroma of the panatelas he occasionally smoked, shaving lotion, and another smell almost like cinnamon, which might be his skin. Her arm, linked in his, pressed into the warmth of his body.

"Is this the news Eugenia heard about first?" she asked slyly, and he told her with a wink that it was. In a few moments she asked, "But would Isabel like to have me there? I thought she seemed uncomfortable with me at times."

"I have already spoken with Isabel," he assured her. "Naturally she was thrown into confusion by your visit, because already she knew that it was no ordinary visit. Much of that was because she wanted to make a good impression on you and didn't know how. But she agrees with me that you would be ideal . . . for the teaching position."

"I'm glad to know that," Catherine said, matching his high seriousness. As they stepped onto the escalator she looked back and saw the owner of the souvenir shop standing stolidly in her doorway. The woman's eyes brushed over Catherine and César, taking no interest in them. Catherine said, "I bought some things in that shop this afternoon. So much has happened since then that I'm surprised that the world doesn't show a change."

"The change is in you," he smiled. "You look radiant."

As they made their way across the waiting room, César pointed to a display of travel posters. "The job does call for some traveling," he said, "and we will begin with wherever you want to go. Of course I would like to take you to Bogotá to meet some of the family, and then there is San Andrés to visit and other places that mean something to me. We will see them all."

"What is your favorite spot in all the world?"

200

Catherine asked him. "The place that makes you the happiest."

After a moment's thought he replied, "Los Limonares is, I suppose, where I am most myself and most at home."

"Then that is where I want to begin," Catherine decided. "With your beginning."

"A modest start but a sound one," he agreed.

Outside they walked to the end of the sidewalk and crossed to a parking lot. When they had found the car, several rows over, Catherine peered inside and asked, "But where is Leonardo?"

"I have to admit," César smiled, "that I was in such a hurry that I drove myself. I do have a few basic skills." He unlocked the door for Catherine, then turned back to her and took her in his arms. "I forgot to mention," he said easily, "that you will be under contract. It is a contract in perpetuity with no options. Will you accept, Catherine Gray, and be my wife?"

Then while she was trying to think, he kissed her and she couldn't think; but of course she didn't need to, anyway. Nestled in his arms in the heart of the tropical night, she felt his hand stroke her hair and heard him say, "This is the miracle that I told you about that day in the rain at Los Limonares, that I found someone to love when and where I least expected to. But then one is never prepared for love's arrival."

"I love you, too, César," she whispered into his shoulder and felt his muscles relax momentarily, as in relief, and then he embraced her tighter.

When they were in the car traveling back toward Cali, Catherine asked, "What happened to the explaining I was supposed to do? Don't I have to tell you about Frank Gibson or what I decided to do about Alex, my fiancé?"

"It doesn't matter," César returned carelessly. "You can tell me whatever you think you should. But I don't think you have any revelations that would change my mind and I'm really not interested in those fellows."

"Well!" Catherine teased. "Not interested in your rivals? I can see your arrogance hasn't diminished."

César laughed. "You are not so humble either. With such parents for models, our children will be absolutely insufferable."

Far, far in the distance, a hazy glow on the horizon announced the location of the city. Catherine arched her back against the seat like a cat and stretched voluptuously. All of the tension of the day had vanished, leaving her light and free. All at once she sat up with a jolt. "Oh, no! My luggage! It's on the plane!"

But César continued without slackening speed. "Haven't I heard something like this before?" he inquired. "It seems to me that the last time I came to the airport I met a pretty girl who had lost a suitcase and I was able to be of some help. So now you are back where you started, Catherine, except for one thing. This time the holiday will last for the rest of your life."

Love—the way you want it!

Candlelight Romances

Once you've tasted joy and passion, do you dare dream of

LOVING

Danielle Steel

bestselling author of
The Promise and *To Love Again*

Bettina Daniels lived in a gilded world—pampered, adored, adoring. She had youth, beauty and a glamorous life that circled the globe—everything her father's love, fame and money could buy. Suddenly, Justin Daniels was gone. Bettina stood alone before a mountain of debts and a world of strangers—men who promised her many things, who tempted her with words of love. But Bettina had to live her own life, seize her own dreams and take her own chances. But could she pay the bittersweet price?

A Dell Book $2.75 (14684-4)

The first novel in the spectacular new
Heiress series

The English Heiress

Roberta Gellis

Leonie De Conyers—beautiful, aristocratic, she lived in the
shadow of the guillotine, stripped of everything she held
dear. Roger St. Eyre—an English nobleman, he set out to save
Leonie in a world gone mad.

They would be kidnapped, denounced and brutally separated. Driven by passion, they would escape France, return
to England, fulfill their glorious destiny and seize a lofty
dream.

A Dell Book $2.50 (12141-8)